Last Chance Wedding

Last Chance Ranch Book 3

Liz Isaacson

ISBN-13: 978-1638761471

Chapter One

J eri Bell whistled as she put on her tool belt, the cheery California sunshine lighting the day beyond her bedroom window. The days she didn't get to work on a construction site were a waste of time in her opinion, and she'd had a lot of those lately.

"But not anymore," she said to herself as she started gathering her copious amounts of hair into a ponytail. She knew most women would kill to have as much hair as she did, especially as hers held a curl like it was the eighties and it hadn't gotten the memo.

Now, she worked at Last Chance Ranch, and they needed dozens of buildings built or remodeled. She was working on the new dog enclosures first, because that would allow Scarlett and the ranch more room to house more animals. And more animals was good for the partnership they had with Forever Friends, who provided a lot of grant money for the ranch.

In fact, Forever Friends provided the salary Jeri had named, right down to the penny. Of course, she'd given an even dollar amount, so there were no pennies. She grinned at herself, burying the vein of guilt that was open and never seemed to close.

She brushed it aside like she'd been doing for a few months now, since she'd come to the ranch and started surveying the land, putting in quotes, and beginning the construction.

Her crew was usually at least a dozen men, and she'd become extraordinarily good at managing them over the past twenty years of her life. But out here, it was her and whichever cowboy she could scrounge from his regular chores if there was something that required more than two hands.

That was almost always Hudson, Scarlett's boyfriend, or Sawyer, the cowboy who lived right next door to her. Jeri looked south as if she had superpowers and could see through cabin walls to the cowboy's place next door.

He had an amazing dog that followed him around the ranch like, well, a puppy, and Jeri mourned the loss of her canine. The chickens she'd brought with her hardly counted as pets, as one of them had a crazy eye that seemed to look everywhere but where it was going. Still, she loved Spot and Feathers, and she left her ponytail to be bumpy so she could go feed them before she hurried over to the construction site.

Her yard wasn't fenced, but the chickens never seemed

to stray too far from the source of their food, and Jeri found them at the bottom of the steps just outside the back door, clucking away.

"Hey, guys," she said, reaching for the wooden lid on the box she'd built to keep the feed in. She grabbed a handful and scattered it over the grass near them. Spot did his funky chicken run as he went after the food.

She laughed at them and threw more feed than they needed. Feathers, a brown and black chicken, would try to follow her over to the construction site. Then she'd realize that it was way too far for her two short feet, and she'd eventually make her way back to the yard.

"I'm going to get that house finished," she promised them, looking at the half-finished coop Scarlett had given her permission to build. "I am. Tonight. I'll work on it tonight."

She was usually exhausted by the time she finished over in Canine Club, and really, she was never finished. She worked until her back ached and she reached a spot where she could pick up the next day. But by the time she got home, she was lucky to stick something in the microwave and collapse on the couch after eating it.

So her diet wasn't the best. She often skipped breakfast and lunch, drinking only water so she didn't faint in the summer heat as she hammered and measured and nailed.

While she worked a lot, she hadn't lost much weight, because her eating habits crammed all her calories—high-density ones—into one meal.

3

It was fine. It was her life again, and she was grateful for that. In fact, she thought, *Thank you for bringing me here* as she walked away from the chickens and around to the dirt road in front of her cabin. She couldn't help glancing at Sawyer's front door, where sometimes the cowboy sat on the steps with his Australian shepherd at his feet and his guitar balanced against the post holding up the porch.

Whenever he sat outside at night and played, Jeri would make sure her windows were open. A few times she'd even gone out onto her back porch and listened to him sing in his beautiful tenor voice.

So maybe she had a little crush on the cowboy next door. Maybe.

Her heart pumped out an extra beat, and she reminded herself that she had done the boyfriend thing. The husband thing. The family thing. The in-a-new-relationship-with-someone-she-worked-with thing.

And she wasn't going to do any of it again.

The price was too high—and she knew. She'd lost everything over the years, and she could only count on herself to rebuild her life.

Which is what I'm doing, she thought as she caught sight of Hudson's truck rounding the corner and coming toward her. She put a smile on her face and waved to him as he passed, because through her divorce, the loss of her business, her crew, and all of her friends, she'd learned that it was easier to smile than to frown.

Scarlett had often said how much she appreciated how

bubbly and optimistic Jeri was around the ranch, and Jeri appreciated the comments. She wasn't exactly faking, but she did like looking at the bright side of things more than the dark. The glass was half-full and not half-empty.

After all, she'd picked herself up from some pretty awful things. Things she didn't want to think about right now.

No, right now, she needed to get the inside walls of the third dog enclosure up. When the structures were finished, they'd be temperature regulated, but right now they weren't. She worked through the morning, sweating and replacing the fluids with as much water as her stomach and bladder could hold.

She knew it was lunch only because the sun shone directly overhead—and Scarlett brought her a chicken Caesar salad.

Something was up. The owner was nice, and Jeri considered Scarlett a friend. Probably the best female friend Jeri had ever had. But she didn't bring Jeri food very often, so Jeri asked, "What's going on?" as she took the salad and the plastic fork from her boss.

Scarlett sighed and looked around the enclosure. "Wow, it's hot in here."

"Yeah," Jeri said, opening the salad and pouring the dressing over it. "Thanks for getting this. Why'd you go down to town?"

"I was meeting with Jewel."

Jeri stuffed her mouth full of lettuce and parmesan so she could buy herself some time to answer.

Liz Isaacson

"She wants to make sure all of our paperwork is up to date," Scarlett said.

"And you need my license," Jeri said, licking her fork like there wasn't a problem. She could produce her non-existent contractor's license in a jiffy. No big deal.

Except it was a big deal. Her application had been turned down again, and the salad suddenly tasted sour. An image of her former foreman filled her mind—Brenden Evans. If she could just get a hearing with the committee, she could give her side of the story.

But she already had, and they'd still taken her license away.

The only way she could get a new license was to use a different name. But she needed legal documentation with the name, and the only way to get that was to lie, or pay for forged documents, or get married.

She couldn't do the first two, because she didn't need to go to jail on top of everything else. She still went to church every chance she got, and she'd begged the Lord for a solution that was legal and would allow her to keep building this life at Last Chance Ranch.

If she could find someone willing to marry her just for a few months....

Just like all the other times she'd thought about this exact thing, no one came to mind. Most sane men didn't just marry female carpenters for a favor.

"I'll go check on the status of it tomorrow," Jeri said, forking another bite of chicken and lettuce into her mouth.

She chewed and swallowed. "Maybe I did something wrong."

"We just need the application and where it is," Scarlett said, still looking around. "This is going so great, Jeri."

She put that smile on her face, nodded, and said, "Thanks." She stirred her salad around, the ever-present guilt blooming and growing into a raging river in her system.

She knew the status of her contractor license, and all she could do was apply again. Make up a little white lie about how she'd done something wrong and had to re-file, and give Scarlett that application status.

It would buy her another few weeks, at least.

Scarlett said goodbye and left the half-finished enclosure, leaving Jeri to her worries and doubts. She couldn't eat any more salad—number one, she disliked salad. Number two, she wasn't used to eating in the middle of the day.

She got back to work. Decided to stop while it was still light—and before she lopped off a thumb because she couldn't focus. Her mind hadn't stopped circling her problem, and she still had no idea what to do about it.

Her stomach growled as she walked back to the main road and around to the Cabin Community. Her feet crunched against the gravel, and she went through every able-bodied man she knew. Before the disaster that had lost her the license, she would've had a crew of fifteen men she could ask for a favor like this.

Now, while she liked this life a lot, she didn't have

anyone the way she used to. No one to really call on in a sticky situation like the one she currently found herself in.

Loneliness engulfed her, and she turned down the driveway that led to her back yard when she heard the clucking.

Up the steps her feet took her, and she went in the front door, her thoughts turning to dinner and what she had in the freezer. Three steps inside the cabin, she realized something was very wrong.

This didn't smell like her house.

"Hullo, Jeri," a man said, causing her to yelp and spin toward the sound. Her heart banged against her ribs as she realized she wasn't staring at an enemy, but Sawyer Smith.

She'd gone in the wrong house. She scanned him from head to toe, noticing his hair was damp and curling in a very sexy way around his ears. He looked totally different without that cowboy hat on his head, and every female part in Jeri started rejoicing that she'd made this particular mistake.

Chapter Two

"Sawyer," Jeri said, scanning him again, and Sawyer felt like he'd put his shirt on backward. Checked and everything. His clothes looked right, zipper was zipped up, all of that.

"I was just thinking," she said, her voice like music to his ears. "I guess I came in the wrong house." Her wide eyes softened, and she laughed, driving Sawyer's thoughts into a frenzy.

He's been texting with his mother about the family picnic at his childhood home in Newport Beach, and she'd been pressing him about who he was bringing. As if showing up to a family event alone wouldn't be tolerated.

Of course, for his family, it wasn't. He'd taken so many women to events, it was a miracle he hadn't simply kept one of them as a girlfriend.

"It's fine," he said, chuckling with her. "I did just

shower, but I'm dressed, obviously." Why was he talking about showering? His face heated, and he didn't say he'd only gotten in the shower so he wouldn't be able to text.

He'd prayed for a solution to his problem, and the next thing he knew, Jeri had walked in his house. Was she the answer to his family situation? Would she be willing to drive a couple of hours south for some bad potato salad and an overcooked hamburger?

Why couldn't he ask her?

He'd asked probably half a dozen other women to stand in as his girlfriend in the past.

Probably because you'd like to take her out for real, he thought.

"Obviously," she said, her eyes still crinkled with laughter. He sure did like her jovial attitude and hardworking spirit. He'd lived next door to her for just over three weeks, and he'd already asked out another woman here and been turned down.

Sort of. Adele was dating Carson, but Sawyer hadn't realized that when he'd asked her to dinner. Was Jeri dating someone he didn't know about?

He didn't know, and he wasn't going to ask. He hadn't dated anyone seriously for a long time, but he knew there were some rules to dating and asking point blank if someone had a girlfriend wasn't how it was done.

"You want to stay for dinner?" he asked. "I put one of those frozen enchilada meals in when I got home."

"Oh, I don't need to do that," she said, turning back to the door. "I'm sure I have pizza or something in my freezer."

"So you could eat my freezer food just as easily as yours," he said, wondering if that was obvious enough for her. Heat spiraled through his body, his air conditioning struggling to keep up with the hot California summer as it was.

No matter what, he didn't want her to leave quite yet. He wanted to go to the picnic, if only to get off the ranch for a couple of days. He loved Last Chance Ranch, he did. But he'd been here for seven years, and sometimes he missed the beach, a society where there were more people than animals, and a faster pace of life.

He'd left horse racing for a reason, and he reminded himself of it each time he started to feel antsy on the ranch. His parents lived only a couple of hours away, and it was the perfect distance for a weekend trip to remind himself of how much he loved the quiet peace of the foothills where the ranch was located.

"I guess," Jeri said, something sparking between them. He wasn't sure what it was. He'd waved to Jeri loads of times. Spoken to her and admired her beauty from thirty yards away, standing on his porch while she stood on hers.

She'd never given him any indication that she was interested in him—or anyone really. Sawyer had lived on the earth long enough to know that everyone had a story, a past, especially when they got to be as old as him and Jeri.

Not that he even know how old she was. He wanted to

find out, and his fingers tingled in anticipation as he moved into the kitchen to check on his pre-made dinner. They could spend hours together in the truck, getting to know one another, as they drove down to Newport Beach.

"Looks like it's almost done," he said, though he had no idea. The timer said ten minutes, so he figured it *was* almost done. "How are the chickens?"

"Just fine," she said, glancing around. "Where's Blue?"

"Oh, he's outside somewhere," Sawyer said, unconcerned. "Hudson was saddling up, and he thought maybe he'd go with him." Sawyer grinned at her, suddenly self-conscious about the state of his cabin. He wasn't the neatest man on the planet, and now every item that sat out of place bothered him.

He opened a drawer and swept the dental floss and tape sitting on the counter into it, trying to find something else to ask her about. "So, Jeri, what did you do before you came to the ranch?"

"I owned a construction company," she said, and Sawyer turned around to find her stepping into the kitchen. The cabin was nice, and he was happy for the housing, but it wasn't exactly high-end. He gestured to the dining room table that only had two chairs, and she moved over to it and sat.

"Your own company," he said. "That's great. You don't anymore?"

"No," she said, shaking her head, an edge entering her eyes. "Not anymore."

"I sense a story there."

"Oh, there's a story." She flashed him a smile that only lit her face halfway. How he knew that, he wasn't sure. Oh, yes, he was. He'd been watching her for a while now. "But I don't want to tell it tonight."

"Fair enough," he said. "Maybe you'll tell me another time."

"Sure," she said, but he detected a bit of falseness in her voice.

His phone buzzed, and they both looked at it. "It's my mother," he said, sighing. "She's having a big barbecue this weekend, and she'd bugging me about coming."

"You don't want to go?" Jeri asked.

"I do," Sawyer said slowly, trying to get the words to line up right inside his mouth. "My family is a bit...peculiar."

"All families are," she said. "My nearest sibling is ten years older than me. I'm the caboose baby."

"Wow," he said. "And how old is that?"

Their eyes caught again, and he smiled at her this time as the electricity pulsed between them.

"My older brother, Ricky, is fifty-two."

So she was even older than him, and Sawyer wasn't sure why, but he did like that. "I'm the middle child," he said. "One older sister. One younger brother. Rosie's married with a couple of kids."

The timer on the oven interrupted them, and Sawyer seized the opportunity to walk away from Jeri, trying to center his thoughts. It certainly was easier when she wasn't so close, perfuming the air with sawdust and something floral.

"Anyway," he said. "My mother is...neurotic about significant others." He pulled the pan of enchiladas out of the oven, almost dropping the tented foil lid on the floor in the process.

"Meaning?" Jeri asked, joining him in the kitchen. She opened two cupboards before she found the plates, and she pulled down two.

"Meaning we don't go to family events without a guest. A partner. A...girlfriend." He swallowed, and he couldn't seem to look away from her. She pulled a couple of forks out of the drawer next to the fridge and faced him.

"Are you asking me to be your guest?" Her eyes danced with amusement. "Partner? Girlfriend?" She pealed out another wave of laughter, and Sawyer joined her.

"No, of course not."

"Oh, who'd you ask?"

"I, uh, haven't asked anyone. I probably won't go." His phone buzzed again, and Jeri glanced back to the table where he'd left it.

"That's too bad," Jeri said, retreating out of the kitchen, giving him room to breathe and work. "I kinda like family picnics."

"Do you?" He stared at her. Maybe he'd messed up already. "It's this weekend," he said. "Like, in two days. It's a couple hours of driving. Each way." He wasn't sure why he was trying to talk her out of it instead of into it.

14

"Well, if you can't get anyone else to go, I'm free." She shrugged those sexy shoulders, the purple straps of her tank top covering her bronzed skin in thin strips.

"Let's plan on it then," he said, his throat raw. He kept his eyes down as he served them each a couple of enchiladas. He slid a plate in front of her and sat down in his spot. "We don't have to leave too terribly early. Maybe like nine or ten."

Jeri smiled at him, and Sawyer couldn't believe things had worked out so easily. He hadn't had to make a fool of himself on her front steps, and he could pretend like he didn't have budding feelings for her, the way he'd been doing.

Still, when their eyes met again, that charge roared to life for the third time. Without hesitating, he said, "Maybe we can go to dinner tomorrow night," he said. "Get to know each other better before we have to hold hands in front of my family."

Jeri dropped her fork with a clatter, her eyes widening again. "Hold hands?"

He chuckled, which relieved some of the tension. "Well, it's been a while since I've had a girlfriend, I'll admit. But I'm pretty sure the kids are holding hands still."

She picked up her fork and cut a bite of enchilada. "I mean, I heard you say girlfriend. I guess I just wasn't expecting...." She let her voice trail into silence, and now she wore a calculating look.

"It would just be for an afternoon," he said, his spirits

falling. She didn't like him. The heat between them was just him. One-sided.

A dog barked outside, and he got up to let Blue in. "There you are, bud," he said. "C'mon in."

"Hey, Blue." Jeri let the Australian shepherd come over to her and she scrubbed him down in hello. "Can he eat enchiladas?"

"I'm sure he can," Sawyer said, liking the way she interacted with his dog. He wasn't sure why everything Jeri did seemed dipped in gold, but her feeding Blue a bit of chicken and cheese seriously got Sawyer's heart thumping in his chest.

The conversation moved to happenings around the ranch, and Jeri stayed for another hour before saying, "I've bothered you all night," and getting to her feet.

"It wasn't a bother," Sawyer said, walking her to the front door. He opened it for her and stepped back, grinning at her in what he hoped was a friendly, next-door-neighborly way.

"So dinner tomorrow." She looked up at him, hope shining in her eyes. And she hadn't asked. "I love that bistro on Clover Street. Have you been there?"

"No, ma'am."

She swatted at his bicep, a laugh following. "I may be old, Mister, but I'm not a ma'am."

"You're not old," he said, hoping he still knew how to flirt.

"Older than you, I'm sure."

"A few years," he said, shrugging. "I'm thirty-eight."

She nodded, her smile revealing her pretty white teeth. "What time tomorrow? I tend to get lost on a project and I don't remember to look at a clock."

"Seven?" It had been a *really* long time since he'd been out with someone. Longer than he wanted to admit.

"Sure, seven." She shuffled forward and stepped back. "All right. See you then." She committed to leaving then, and stepped fully out onto the porch.

"Bye," he said as she went down the steps and across the lawn to her house. He sighed and picked up his guitar from its spot just inside the door. For the first time in a very long time, he didn't feel like the evening hours were too long.

His fingers plucked a tune out of the strings without him thinking about it, and he hummed a love song in the back of his throat, his thoughts centered firmly on the beautiful Jeri Bell.

Chapter Three

Jeri pressed her back into the cabin door, her mind spinning. She'd walked into the wrong house. An innocent mistake. At least he'd been dressed, and a small giggled escaped her lips.

"What a great night," she murmured to herself as she wandered down the short hallway to her bedroom. Such a better night than making her own freezer food and passing out on the couch. Not only that, she felt like God had given her another chance when she thought she was plumb out.

"Could he give me his last name?" she wondered aloud as she changed into her pajamas. It wasn't nearly time for bed yet, but Jeri was exhausted. She went back into the kitchen and opened the freezer, taking out the container of chocolate peanut butter ice cream that was still half-full.

The soft sound of strumming drifted through the air, and she went out onto the back steps as she'd done before.

Before, though, she'd simply day-dreamed about holding Sawyer's hand and having him sing to her in that stunning voice. But now, she couldn't stop thinking about asking him to marry her.

Just for a couple of months. She didn't want to be married for good ever again. The thought of telling Sawyer about her first marriage made her muscles seize up. She shook her head. No, she didn't want the marriage to be real or long-lasting.

She just needed proof of a new name so she could apply for her contractor's license again. She was doing him a favor, albeit a much smaller one. Perhaps he could do the same. He didn't seem to get off the ranch much, but she'd only been there a few weeks.

Still, they'd already had a Fourth of July picnic here on the ranch, and he seemed to fit into the group easily. Why he felt like he needed to attend his family's shindig was still a mystery to her.

She was just glad she'd walked into the wrong house at the right time.

After several bites of ice cream, her mind caught up to the last couple of hours. She had a date with the man tomorrow night. A date—she hadn't been on one of those is a very long time. She jumped to her feet and put the ice cream away, because she had much more pressing things to do— figure out what to wear when dining with a sexy cowboy.

Foolishness raced through her as she started leafing through her closet. She certainly didn't have anything worthy of a date with anyone, let alone Sawyer. Secondly, she couldn't allow her tiny crush to manifest itself.

Picking out a clean pair of jeans and a sleeveless blouse in peach with large, splashy flowers on it, she sat down heavily on the bed.

This wasn't going to be real. They were getting off the ranch to learn about each other so they could fake out his family.

"It's not real," she told herself. She didn't want it to be real anyway. She liked her solitary life, and while she missed the camaraderie she'd once had with her crew, she was starting to make new friends here on this ranch.

That was all Sawyer could ever be. A friend.

But maybe the kind of friend who'd marry her so she could get something precious to her—and necessary for the ranch.

Yes, that was how she needed to spin it. If she couldn't provide her license, the ranch would lose funding.

TIME SEEMED to march steadily forward, and before Jeri knew it, she'd finished another day's work on the dog enclosure. She stood in her kitchen probably an hour before she would've normally quit for the day, dressed in that blouse and feeling like someone had dug a pit right through the bottom of her stomach.

She was going to have to tell him things she hadn't told anyone. At least anyone in a long, long time.

It's fine, she thought. She needed a good friend out here, and it might as well be Sawyer. She'd always gotten along better with men than women, though she did like Scarlett, Adele, and Sissy, the new accountant.

But Sissy didn't live on-site and Scarlett and Adele were already thick as thieves.

Jeri's thoughts turned to her past, and she knew she could probably still text Evelyn, the woman who'd ran Jeri's office for her. Everyone had lost their jobs after the accident, but Evelyn, at least, hadn't blamed her.

In fact, out of everyone involved, only Evelyn had testified that Jeri would've never allowed that—

A loud knock on her front door had her gasping and spinning toward the sound. "He's here." Of course he was there. They were going to dinner. She wondered what the other people on the ranch would think when they saw the two of them traipsing off together.

"You're consenting adults," she told herself as she strode across the cabin. She wished she could command her heartbeat to stop sprinting as easily, but it continued to race beneath her breastbone as if it had somewhere to go.

"Hey," she said with a smile, concealing her inner turmoil. "Let me grab my purse and I'll be ready."

Sawyer stood with his head bent, the brim of his cowboy hat concealing his face. He looked up at her, a smile sitting in his eyes and adorning his mouth. He was so good-looking it made her breath catch, and she didn't move to get her purse.

"Evenin', Jeri," he said in a slow, easy voice. "You look great."

She actually looked down at herself to make sure she'd gotten dressed. Of course she had. The peach-colored blouse concealed some of her bulk, and she'd loved the shirt since the moment she'd seen it online.

"Thank you," she murmured, still drinking him in. He'd shaved, and not just his face. His hair had been freshly cut close to his head, and the neat trim extended up under his hat where she couldn't see. So he probably wouldn't have those wet curls around his ears if he removed that delicious hat.

"You need a minute?" he asked, taking a step forward as if he'd come in.

"Yeah," she said, falling back a step. He wore jeans too, and those cowboy boots, and a button-up shirt in lavender.

Lavender.

He was downright dangerous to her health, and as he moved past her, she almost swooned at the scent of his cologne. "Your place is just like mine," he said, grinning at her.

"Well, not quite," she said, coming to her senses. "I've got a birthday cake candle burning pretty much non-stop."

He chuckled, the sound tickling her eardrums and making her smile. She swiped her purse from the side table near the couch and pronounced herself ready.

He gestured for her to go first out the front door, and she glanced left and right as if she wanted to make a clean getaway. Directly across from her cabin in the U-shaped community was Cache Bryant's cabin. He was brand new to the ranch, as was David Merrill, who'd moved in a few days ago.

"How are the new guys settling in?" she asked as she went around to the passenger side of Sawyer's truck.

"Just fine," he said, darting in front of her to open the door. She glanced at him, that explosive heat between them manifesting itself. She had no idea if he felt any of the same things she did, but in that moment, time slowed.

She stared into his eyes, and she saw the desire radiating within him.

Time rushed forward again, and she climbed into the cab of the truck, fear taking a tight grip of her heart.

Sawyer liked her.

Of course he likes me, Jeri thought in a stern voice. *I'm very likable.* That was one thing her mother had always told her. She didn't need siblings close to her age, because she could make friends so easily.

She watched the cowboy she'd been crushing on circle the front of the vehicle and climb in beside her. The atmosphere in the truck felt like it had been plugged into to a high-voltage source, and Jeri's voice stayed dormant beneath her thoughts.

She liked him too. Could he see it? Feel it?

Maybe it'll make things easier, she thought, almost

scoffing along with it. She wasn't an expert in relationships, heaven knew that. Her first marriage had been a complete disaster, and her ex-husband had taken their son and cut Jeri out of everything.

No matter what, she knew emotions and having feelings for someone made everything a whole lot harder.

"So you said your nearest brother was a decade older than you," Sawyer said. "Other siblings?"

"Yeah," Jeri said, her voice creaky. She cleared her throat. "My oldest sister is sixty. Molly lives near our mother in Glendale. She moved there after my dad died a few years ago."

"I'm sorry," Sawyer said.

"Yeah," Jeri said again, though she didn't miss her father all that much. She'd loved him, of course. But she'd lived her whole life feeling like the Bell family had been complete before she'd arrived. She pushed the thoughts away, because she didn't like the way they poisoned her outlook on life.

Her parents had taken good care of her growing up. They loved her, she knew that.

"Wilma is fifty-five. She's living in Temecula right now."

"Oh, Southern California," he said.

"I don't get why you'd live in California if you weren't near the beach," Jeri said. "But she seems to like it there."

"It's a nice area," he said.

"And your family is from Newport Beach?" she asked, though her memory from last night was perfect.

"Yep," he said, taking them past the robot mailbox—

Prime—that stood guard at the entrance to the ranch. "Both of my siblings live in the area still."

"So you're the loner," she said with a smile.

He threw one at her too. "I suppose so."

"That's okay," she said. "I am too."

He gave her a curious look then, and Jeri felt like worlds had started colliding. She saw herself sharing a lot with this man, and that scared her, scared her, scared her.

"So family stuff is out of the way," he said. "Brother Ricky. Sisters Wilma and Molly."

"Right." She reminded herself this was for show. He needed to know the basics so they could survive the picnic. Nothing more.

Nothing more, she commanded herself. *Except maybe marriage.*

She smiled at the extra thought—but not because she actually wanted to marry Sawyer. Oh, no. That wasn't why.

She needed her license. The ranch needed funding. And maybe, just maybe, she needed a friend too.

A *friend.*

Nothing more.

Chapter Four

They'd seen nobody in the Cabin Community and didn't pass anyone on the short five-minute drive down to town.

"What are your brother's and sister's names again?" Jeri asked, and Sawyer wondered if he'd told her last night or not. Honestly, since she'd walked in his cabin like she owned it, his thoughts had been scattered at best.

"James and Rosie."

"James and Rosie," she repeated. "That's right. Rosie's married with a couple of kids."

"Right," he said. "Both boys. "Ambrose and Oliver." He cut a glance at her to see how she felt about the names. "She has a bit of a fetish with all things England."

"Hey," Jeri said with a shrug. "To each her own."

"What do you like?" he asked, hoping it really was okay

to get to know her tonight. His mother wouldn't ask too many embarrassing questions, but he at least had to know something about her. He couldn't just show up and say, "This is my next-door neighbor, Jeri...what was your last name again?"

That would definitely open the floodgates for questions —questions he didn't want to deal with. Questions he'd answered before, but obviously not to anyone's satisfaction but his own. Which was fine. He didn't have to justify to anyone why he'd left horse racing.

"Oh, boy," Jeri said, blowing her breath out. "What do I like? That's a really broad question."

"Let's start with food," he said.

"Mashed potatoes," she said instantly. "And chocolate muffins. My mother had a killer chocolate muffin recipe."

"Sounds good," he said, his stomach pinching. He did not normally eat this late at night, but he knew Jeri did. She worked past seven most nights, and Sawyer admired her drive.

"And you?" she asked. "Besides boxed enchiladas, of course."

"Let's see," he said, turning and keeping his attention on the road. "My favorite food would have to be roast beef sandwiches."

"A man after my heart," she said with a laugh, and Sawyer joined right in with her, thinking this was going to be the best date he'd been on, ever. Everything with Jeri was so easy, and he loved that about her.

After all, everything with Calissa had been so hard.

He couldn't believe the woman was still in his mind, but he supposed fiancées were hard to eradicate completely, even after they carved out hearts.

He still had a heart, he knew. It drummed in his chest, reminding him how much he liked this woman riding with him in the truck. "Here we are," he said, pulling into the parking lot at the bistro she liked.

"You've never been here?" she asked.

He peered up at the sign that read District 51. "Nope."

"How long have you been at the ranch?" She unbuckled her seat belt and reached for the door handle.

"Seven years," he said as she got out. They met at the front of the truck, and Sawyer wondered if he could take her hand right then. Just sort of see how it fit in his, so tomorrow wouldn't be the first time they touched.

His throat felt like sand, but he moved his hand toward hers anyway. The moment he touched her, fireworks filled his whole body. Jeri pulled in a breath and met his eyes, and Sawyer seriously considered telling her everything he felt.

The moment lasted for about two seconds, and then he gained control of his insane desire to spill all his secrets. Some things should stay hidden for a while, and one of those was his small infatuation with this woman.

They just had a picnic to get through. Then life would go back to normal, and he'd sip coffee on the front porch while she walked down the dirt road to work. That was all.

He certainly wasn't going to have a ranch romance with a woman who wouldn't be staying long-term.

Jeri adjusted her hand in his and smiled at him. "They have great beef barbacoa tacos here," she said. "They have garlic mashed potatoes in them." Her dark eyes sparkled like diamonds, and Sawyer couldn't help himself. His resolve to make this a single weekend relationship slipped, and slipped hard.

"Okay, so my mother's name is Farrah," he said the next day, Jeri next to him on the seat again, driving past the welcoming mailbox robot. "Dad is Taylor." He'd thought of at least a dozen things he should've talked about with Jeri at dinner last night.

He'd completely lost his mind, that was what had happened instead. He let himself think he was on a date with a beautiful woman instead of focusing on prepping her for this family event. And yes, she needed to be prepped.

"Farrah. Taylor," she repeated, murmuring something else under her breath.

"And, joy of joys, I just found out this morning that James has an actual girlfriend." He glanced at Jeri, his nerves shot and they hadn't even left town yet. "Like, a real girlfriend, not someone he's bringing to the picnic to appease our mother."

She met his eye, and Sawyer looked away quickly. He felt like she could see right inside him, and while he kind of liked it, he was afraid of what he was telling her.

"Which means you're the odd one out again," she said.

"Exactly," he said, his frustration boiling up and touching the back of his brain. He hated feeling like this. "Maybe we should just skip this. It's just a dumb picnic on the beach."

"Obviously not," she said. "This is a family tradition. A goodbye to summer, right? Didn't you say you've been doing this beach day-slash-picnic since you were a kid?"

He sighed and looked out his window to check for traffic. "Yeah."

"It'll be fine," she said. "I've had a lot of experience dealing with people."

"Yeah?"

"Oh, yeah," she said. "Twenty-three years in construction will do that to a person. Foreman, owners, land developers. I've sat in more meetings and charmed more people into seeing things my way than I care to admit."

He looked at her, and she didn't seem to be bragging. He wondered if Jeri even could boast about how great she was. She was so...*good*. So down-to-earth.

"Anyway," she said. "I think I can handle your mother."

"She's a special type of person," Sawyer said, his mood darkening again. "And I should probably tell you why my dad and I don't get along."

31

"Oh, story time," she said enthusiastically.

"Yeah, and then you have to tell me one," he said. "Anything. Something light and fun."

"I think I can do that," she said.

"So my dad owns a training company. Horses." Sawyer took a deep breath, trying to decide if he should go for the long version or the short one. "Basically, he works with the best racehorses in the country. Trains them. Takes care of them when they're not on the track. That kind of thing. James still works for him. I don't. That's about it."

"There's so much more than that," Jeri said. "But I see what you're saying. You left the family business."

"Right."

"When?"

"Seven years ago."

"Ah, so you broke later in life." She nodded like another piece of the puzzle had fallen into place. "Do you mind me asking why?"

He did—and he didn't. Someone else, he might not have wanted to tell. But Jeri was so easy to talk to, he found himself saying, "It wasn't the lifestyle I wanted. It might seem glamorous, but it was...too fast-paced for me. Too much living in the shadows. Too many half-truths."

And there was another thing. "My parents aren't religious." He looked at her though he should be watching the freeway ahead of him. "And after I left and came to Last Chance Ranch, I started going to church. I think they...." He exhaled, knowing exactly what they thought, because his dad had shouted it at him five years ago.

"They think I judge them," Sawyer said. "I don't think I do, but there's that between us too." He'd seen her go to church with Scarlett and Hudson, so Sawyer felt he could say such things to her.

Instead of apologizing or saying anything really, Jeri unbuckled her seatbelt and slid across the bench seat until she was thigh-to-thigh with him. The warmth from her body sent shivers right into his bloodstream.

And when she took his hand in hers, gently curling her fingers between his, she said, "That's rough, Sawyer."

His whole soul lit up, and he squeezed her hand. Emotion made a lump form in his throat, and he couldn't speak. Thankfully, he could drive with one hand silently, because that was what he did for the next several minutes.

"I guess I should've told you all of this sooner," he finally said. "You're sort of stuck coming now."

"I want to go," she said quietly, and if Sawyer could've seen her face, he might've known more what she was feeling. She inhaled and added, "So I guess it's my turn. Do you want light and fun or something more along what you just said?"

"Up to you," he said, though he was dying to know more about her. Real things. Deep things. Meaningful things that would bond them together, and maybe carry them into a friendship beyond this weekend.

A real friendship.

Sawyer hadn't had a real friend in a while either. Sure, he counted Gramps, who'd hired him seven years ago. He'd done the best he could with the death of his wife, and Sawyer had tried to keep everything afloat himself or by hiring seasonal workers.

When Scarlett had taken over the ranch, everything had improved drastically, including Sawyer's quality of life.

"I'll do something hard," she said. "It happened a long time ago, but it's always there, in the center of my mind."

Sawyer waited while she took a few seconds to ready herself to speak.

"I was married once," she said, and Sawyer's heart skipped a beat. "It sort of started out as a joke. I mean, that sounds weird, but yeah."

When she didn't continue, Sawyer asked, "How does a marriage start out as a joke?"

"Someone said this friend of mine, Howie, couldn't get anyone to marry him, and I was standing there and said I would. So we did."

"Wow." Sawyer didn't know what to think. Surely there were finer details to the story—all stories had them—but he'd just given her the overview of his long-lasting complications with his family.

"Yeah," Jeri said. "It was spontaneous, and maybe we didn't think things through. Especially when I got pregnant."

Surprise cut right through Sawyer. "You have kids."

34

"Just one," she said. "A son." She grew very quiet, and not just in her voice. She seemed much more subdued in body and spirit, and Sawyer squeezed her hand again.

"What happened?"

"Short version—I left. Howie asked me to leave, and I left. He and Randy—my son—live in Eugene now, and neither of them speak to me."

Sawyer had no idea what to say. This wasn't a hard story. Well, it was, but what he'd really classify it as was sad. Heartbreaking.

"How long?" he asked.

"Uh, let's see." She sighed a long sigh. "I haven't spoken to Howie in seventeen years. Randy about eight now. He's twenty."

So she was young when she'd had him. Young when she'd spontaneously married someone.

He didn't know what to say or do, so he just let his mind work through what it needed to. Without thinking, he lifted her hand to his lips and pressed a kiss to the inside of her wrist. "I'm sorry."

The words weren't adequate, and she didn't answer verbally. She did snuggle into his bicep a bit more, sigh, and close her eyes. Sawyer basked in the warmth from her newfound presence in his life, and he prayed that maybe, just maybe, they could extend their relationship past this picnic.

Guide me, he prayed. *I'll do what Thou would have me do.*

The truck seemed to have a mind of its own, as if it had driven this road to his parents' beachfront property before.

All too soon, Sawyer pulled into the driveway of the mansion where he'd grown up. "All right," he said, facing the front doors as dread filled his stomach. "We're here."

Chapter Five

The level of anxiety in Sawyer's voice wasn't lost on Jeri. She looked at the house in front of her, though mansion was probably a better term for it. It had two garages, enough to hold four cars, and everything about it screamed wealth.

So his family had money. Big deal. Jeri had never really cared all that much about money, though she had worked hard to get recognition among a male-dominated career, worked hard to build her business into a reputable one.

And one mistake—and not even hers—had undone everything she'd scraped and sacrificed to build.

Her determination to ask him—explain to him the situation she was in—hardened. She hadn't known what to do after everything had fallen apart, but she was done letting Brenden dictate what she could do with her life.

"Do we need a code word?" she asked. "You know, in case I get in trouble and need you to come rescue me?"

He looked at her with a hint of surprise. "Yeah, let's do that. I may have forgotten to mention how intense my mother is."

Jeri giggled, though she had gotten that memo. "So... code word. How about—"

"Bird house," he said. "Easy to work into a conversation. There's one right there." He nodded to the designer bird house atop a pole in the flowerbed a few feet from her.

"Bird house. Got it." She glanced at the mansion in front of them, feeling overwhelmed by it and wondering what she'd find through the front door. "Should we go in?"

"I may have forgotten to mention my parents are rich," he said.

"It's just money," she said. "They're just people." She tapped his arm. "Let's go. I see curtains moving inside, and I think we have a matter of seconds before your mother comes out here to get us."

Sawyer turned toward her, his face only a few inches from hers. Everything fell away, and Jeri swallowed, trying to remember the last time she'd kissed a man.

Brenden.

The last man she'd kissed was Brenden, and her heart and life and business had been shredded by that man.

But Sawyer...wasn't Brenden, and Jeri had no business left to lose.

He leaned forward, and for half a second, she thought he'd kiss her. He did, but his lips touched her forehead briefly, and he whispered, "Thank you, and I'm going to apologize in advance."

He twisted and got out of the truck, turning back to help her down. She kept her hand in his as they walked toward the front doors, which opened before they got there.

A shriek filled the air that surely belonged to a much younger woman. But no, it was his mother, and she hurried down the steps to embrace Sawyer.

"Sawwy's here," she said, giggling like a schoolgirl. Jeri thought she might have been wrong. Maybe this woman wasn't just another person.

She stepped back a couple of feet to give Sawyer room to hug his mother. He held her tight, so he obviously loved her. "Hey, Mom," he said, almost in a monotone. Their eyes met, and Sawyer rolled his eyes halfway, a smile on his face.

He cleared his throat and backed out of the embrace. "Mom, this is Jeri Bell." He indicated her, and Jeri felt every inch of her body as his mother sized her up.

Sixteen, Jeri wanted to say. *I wear a size sixteen.*

She extended her hand, her smile painted in place, and said, "So nice to meet you, Farrah."

His mom glanced at Sawyer again before shaking Jeri's hand. "Are you two together?"

"Mom," Sawyer said at the same time Jeri said, "Yes."

She refused to look at him. Too many exchanged glances

always indicated little white lies, and this one wouldn't hurt anyone.

Please don't let it hurt me, she prayed as his mother released her hand. She could easily see herself dating Sawyer, but she knew it wouldn't go anywhere.

She wasn't interested in a long-term relationship. She didn't want another husband, or even a boyfriend. So Sawyer was dark and dreamy and made her heart pitter in a way it hadn't for a while.

Didn't mean she wanted a more complicated life than she currently had. She just wanted someone to talk to that wasn't covered in feathers. To get the job done at Last Chance Ranch. After that, she'd rebuild all she'd lost when Brenden had made a mistake, caused a serious accident, and blamed everything on her.

So her future wasn't even at Last Chance Ranch. A relationship with Sawyer couldn't be long-term. Surely he knew that too. So why was he looking at her with those devastating eyes, that flirty smile on his face?

Maybe Jeri needed to stop thinking long-term. Maybe she should just enjoy this day with him, get him to lend her his last name, and take it one day at a time.

She focused on the conversation, especially when a dark-haired woman joined them in front of the house. Clearly Sawyer's sister, Rosie said, "Come on inside. You're letting in all the heat."

"Yes, let's go inside," his mother said, and Sawyer

grabbed Jeri's hand before they followed her up the few steps.

"Thank you," he whispered into her hair, and Jeri cuddled right into his side, deciding right then and there to enjoy every minute with him.

She met his father, and his brother, and his two nephews. It became clear quickly that his mother was the source of all the tension in the room, and almost everyone tiptoed around her.

Jeri went over to her in the kitchen, where she was putting the finishing touched on the deviled eggs. "Sawyer says you guys did some remodeling in the back yard."

Farrah looked up, a hint of surprise in her eyes. "We did. Would you like to see it?"

"Absolutely," Jeri said. "I don't know if Sawyer's said much about me—we just started dating recently—but I'm a general contractor."

Part horror and part shock filled her expression. "Well, isn't that nice?" Code for *That is not nice. Please stop dating my son.*

Jeri smiled at her and tucked her hair behind her ear. "Sawyer says you and Taylor own some horses," she continued as she followed Farrah around the huge island and out the double French doors to the covered patio.

"Oh, not here," Farrah said, and Jeri paused to take in the huge expanse of the ocean in front of her.

"This view is amazing," she gushed, the sunlight glinting on the waves. Sawyer had not mentioned that his parents had beachfront property, just like he'd forgotten to mention the mansion and the money.

"Isn't it?" Farrah sighed and cocked her perfect size-six hip while she too gazed out at the ocean. "We have private access, but we won't go down until we eat."

Jeri looked at Farrah, a sliver of self-consciousness squirreling through her. She'd never given much thought to her curves, though she knew she carried a few more pounds than other women.

"When will we be eating?" she asked.

"Oh, not for an hour or so," Farrah said, and Jeri's hopes dropped all the way to the beach below them.

She managed to push out a girly laugh anyway, and then Farrah started showing her the new pool and hot tub, the gazebo, and the stepping stones the grandsons had made with their baby hand and footprints in them.

Farrah could talk, and talk, and talk, which was just fine with Jeri. She accepted the bottle of water Sawyer's mother offered her from the outdoor kitchen—who needed an outdoor kitchen only thirty feet from their regular kitchen?

Jeri put on an excellent performance, a little thrill moving through her when Sawyer took her hand again to walk with her down to the beach. His father carried a huge picnic basket, complete with the red checkered blanket.

Rosie's husband wheeled the cooler behind them, and everyone else carried a beach chair for themselves. Sawyer carried his and Jeri's, and she liked his chivalry.

Blankets got spread out on the sand and food taken out

of the basket. The conversation was easy out under the open sky, and the laughter flowed from the little boys and their grandfather.

Sawyer's brother had brought his real girlfriend, and James and Peach were friendly and open, while being cute and obviously infatuated with each other. Jeri wondered if she and Sawyer acted that way, and she liked that he brought her food, and sat next to her and held her hand.

He was a man of few words, but she caught him looking at her a few times, even behind his sunglasses, and wow, he was as attractive with the short hair and shades as he was in the cowboy hat and boots.

"You having fun?" he asked.

"Yeah," she said honestly. "This is great." She scanned the sand in front of her. "I didn't bring a swimming suit, but I want to go in the ocean." She grinned at him, turning on as much flirtyness as she could muster. "You up for it?"

Surprise emanated from him, but he only hesitated for a moment before pushing himself up. "Let's go."

She let him pull her to her feet, and she kicked her flip flops onto the blanket in front of them. Giggling, she walked with him, their fingers intertwined as they walked through the sand.

"I haven't been to the beach in so long," she said, tipping her head back and letting the warmth of the sun hit her full in the face.

"I only come when I visit my parents."

"I can see why," she said. "Private beachfront, only a few flights from the back yard."

Sawyer tipped his head toward her. "Probably should've told you about that."

"Probably," she said. "But it's fine. They're nice. I like them."

"They like you too," he said. "Which is weird." He looked back over his shoulder at where the rest of his family sat.

"Gee, thanks," Jeri said, stung by his words.

"That's not what I meant," Sawyer said quickly. "You're great. You're really great with people, and I'm not even sure my mom's human."

Jeri sent a peal of laughter up into the sky. "I thought the same thing when I first met her. But you just have to get her talking about something she's interested in. It's butter from there."

"Butter." Sawyer chuckled, stumbled in the sand and stepped away from her before bringing her close again. "Thanks for doing this."

"You've got to stop saying thank you," she said. "I volunteered." Could she get him to volunteer to stand before a pastor and say I do?

Jeri's next step brought her to the wet, hard-packed sand, and she was only moments away from the ocean. It was huge and wonderful and she loved it.

Before she could feel the cool water rush over her feet, she paused and pulled on Sawyer's arm. "I have something I should tell you too," she said, hoping her explanation and subsequent favor didn't ruin their day.

"Yeah?" he asked, gazing down at her. Haloed with the sun as he was, he was absolutely gorgeous, and Jeri felt the words dry up right inside her mouth.

"Yeah," she said, but she couldn't get the words to come out. "I'll save story time for the way home, though. Come on, let's dip our feet in."

THE TIME PASSED QUICKLY, and before Jeri knew it, she sat on the bench seat with Sawyer at her side, her hand in his, and the miles passing underneath his tires quickly.

Too quickly.

Darkness took forever to fall in the summer, and she couldn't rely on him not being able to see her while she explained anything.

The silence between them was comfortable, and she didn't want to ruin it. However, her time was running out if she wanted to explain much of anything.

"I have a favor to ask," she started, wishing she'd begun a different way.

"Go ahead," he said. "I owe you one."

"This one is a little bit bigger than an afternoon with your family." Jeri didn't want to ask him this way. Why had she started like that?

He waited for her to speak, but Jeri couldn't seem to find the words.

Start with the ranch, she told herself, and she forced a laugh out of her mouth. "I think I got ahead of myself. So Scarlett hired me to do a bunch of construction at the ranch, right?"

"Yeah," he said. "Projected to take until February, I heard."

"Yes," she said, seizing onto the facts of the job. The job she needed. It was months and months of work, and she loved the ranch. "And I need to provide my contractor's license for Forever Friends to keep funding the ranch, and the thing is...."

He glanced at her. "The thing is...."

She drew in a big breath. "The thing is, I don't have my contractor's license right now." The words poured out of her now. "I lost it when my business went under, and they won't give me another one. But if I could apply under a different name, then I could get one, and Scarlett wouldn't have to know, and the funding for the ranch would be fine." She ran out of air and sucked in another lungful of oxygen.

"How are you going to apply under a different name?" he asked, clearly not connecting the dots.

"Well," she started. "I'd need to get married."

"Married?" Sawyer jerked the wheel as he twisted toward her. He righted the vehicle quickly, and this silence certainly wasn't comfortable.

"Just think about it," Jeri said. "It wouldn't be real. A

make-believe marriage. For a few months. Just for the ranch." She tried to believe her own words, but they sounded a bit, well, make-believe to her.

"A make-believe marriage," he repeated, shock in his voice. He looked at her again. "Dear Lord, you're not kidding."

"No," she said, shaking her head. "I'm not."

Chapter Six

S awyer arrived at the church forty-five minutes before the service was scheduled to start. He sat in the back of the chapel, where he usually slid a minute or two before the pastor stood up to speak.

Today, though, he really needed some answers.

Jeri's proposal—and he used that term literally—felt utterly insane to him. He understood the basic premise, even though she'd gone on to explain a lot more. She'd come inside his cabin instead of going inside hers, and she'd shown him the newspaper articles about the accident at her build site.

She'd told him a story—a long one—about a man named Brenden Evans, her former foreman and the cause of the accident. But she, as owner, had taken the fall. And it was a hard fall, and a long fall, and Sawyer knew she was still picking up all the pieces.

The nice-guy side of him wanted to help her. His first instinct had been to say *yes, sure, let's go to City Hall on Monday morning.*

But he'd been so startled that he'd just listened. Looked at all the pictures. Read the articles. And now, he was in the chapel to pray.

There were so many pieces up in the air, and he just needed to get them all in line. He started with the bottom line—he liked Jeri. So maybe that colored all the other pieces. Made them warp and change shape while they were still in midair.

But he liked Jeri.

He liked Jeri a lot. And he wanted her to stay at the ranch for as long as possible. A small part of him thought that if she'd stay, she'd fall in love with him and start to build her business just five minutes down from the ranch in Pasadena.

Fool, he thought, but the word softened almost immediately. He wasn't being a fool. He was here, wasn't he? Trying to figure out what God would want him to do?

Of course, his father would think praying was a very foolish thing to do. His visit to his parents yesterday had been the best he'd had in years, and he knew why. Jeri.

It seemed a lot of things in his life right now came down to Jeri.

So what do I do? he prayed, his eyes drifting closed.

The earth didn't shake, and no lights flashed from heaven. But Sawyer felt calm and peaceful, which usually meant that whatever thought had entered his head was okay with God. He'd felt like this when he'd decided to leave the horse training business his dad had inherited from his father, and his father from his.

It had been one of the most difficult decisions he'd ever made, but he'd prayed about it and he'd felt exactly as he did now. Peaceful. Calm. Like no matter what happened next, he'd be okay, because the Lord was in control.

"So say yes?" he asked, thinking about what his life would be like if he really married Jeri. Would they live next door to each other? Tell anyone? Pretend like their feelings weren't real?

A make-believe marriage.

Sawyer actually thought he could do that—if he didn't have real feelings for Jeri. And he'd been out of the dating pool for a while, but it sure seemed like the attraction between him and Jeri definitely flowed both ways. It would actually be easier if it didn't.

He pulled out his phone and sent Jeri a quick text. *I need more info. Can we talk?*

Of course. When?

Now. I'm at the church. Maybe we could skip today?

I can meet you wherever, whenever.

His heart took courage, and it started beating a little faster too. He got up from the pew in the back row and headed outside. *I'll come pick you up then. Ten minutes.*

See you then.

Sawyer drove slowly, unsure of why he needed a few

more minutes before he faced Jeri when he'd specifically asked to see her. Eventually, though, with all the right turns, he pulled up to her cabin and found her sitting on the front steps.

When she saw his truck, she jumped up, and the sight of her further calmed him. She was beautiful, with those dark curls falling over her shoulders and halfway down her arms. She wore sunglasses, as she usually did during the day. A pair of black shorts paired with a blue sleeveless shirt that made everything about her seem brighter and more beautiful.

She was his sky—the same color as her shirt—and Sawyer wanted to jump from the truck and gather her into a hug. She reached the door and got in the vehicle before he could even move.

"Hey," she said, her voice a little more timid than normal. She tucked her hair behind her ear and buckled her seatbelt. "Are we just driving?"

"We can do whatever," he said.

"Let's go to Universal Studios," she said. "You want to?"

No, Sawyer did not want to. But it was only about a half an hour away, and maybe he'd have fun at a theme park when he was with Jeri. He put the truck in gear and eased around the U-shaped road to get back to the exit.

"So you said you needed more information," she said.

"Yeah," he said, wishing he knew what kind of information. But he only knew what he knew. "I guess I'm just wondering about the living situation if we do this."

"Oh," she said, her voice full of surprise. "Well...I have my cabin and you have yours."

"So we're not telling anyone about this marriage."

"No," she said. "It's just for paperwork purposes. I can get my license back, and keep my job, and make sure the ranch keeps its funding *and* gets the buildings it needs." She looked at him with desperation in her dark eyes, and Sawyer thought he'd do anything to make it go away.

In fact, he was about to.

"All right," he said. "I'll marry you."

A yelp came out of her mouth. She slapped a hand over it. "Are you serious?" Her wide eyes were beautiful, and Sawyer felt like an idiot for thinking so.

This was going to be fake. Not real.

And yet, his heart beat wildly in a very real way. And his fantasies really wanted to become real. And his feelings felt very, very real.

"I'm serious," he said. "We can go down and do it tomorrow."

"Um," she said. "Sort of."

"Sort of?" He glanced at her.

"Yeah, I did some research last night. We can apply online for a marriage license, but we need to make an appointment to get married." Her voice trailed off. "This is insane, right?"

"It's a little crazy," he said. "But I believe you about the accident, and I don't want you to leave the ranch—" He cut off, because he was about to say way too much. Real things, not make-believe things.

She watched him for a moment, and then she unbuckled and slid across the seat, tucking her arm through his. "I don't want to leave the ranch either." She looked at him, the weight of her eyes heavy on the side of his face. "And not just because I need the job."

He cleared his throat. "So...an appointment?"

"Yeah." She gave herself a little shake. "They're on Wednesdays or Fridays, and we need to call and set something up. Has to be an hour before closing, and we have fifteen days to use the marriage license."

"So Wednesday," he said. "Didn't you say you needed it quickly?"

"Yes," she said. "If possible."

"It's possible," he said. "Where do we have to go?"

"The closest office is in Van Nuys."

Sawyer just drove, thinking seventy-two hours ahead to Wednesday. He could do this.

"It'll just be a couple of months," she said. "Then I'll be out of your hair." She reached up and touched the back of his neck, curling her hand along his shoulders. "Not that you have much hair." She giggled, and Sawyer wanted to tell her everything he was feeling.

He bit back the words. "However long is fine," he said. "It's not like I have a lot of prospects for dates up at the ranch."

"That's not true," Jeri said. "Scarlett has the new

accountant, and she just hired a marketing executive too. She moved into the cabin next to Adele."

Sawyer automatically rejected both women. He'd met Sissy, and she was nice. Dark-haired like Jeri. But she wasn't Jeri. He hadn't met the marketing executive yet, but she didn't sound like his type.

"Are you going to set me up with someone else?" he teased. "Your husband?"

She laughed, and Sawyer sure liked the sound of it. If marrying her would keep her close to him and let him start to break down some of her walls, it was just another reason to do it.

"So separate living conditions," he said. "Are there any perks to this job?"

She laughed again, but the thing was, Sawyer wasn't kidding. And the way she held his hand, and sat beside him, and flirted with him?

She wanted the perks a marriage brought too. Satisfied with that knowledge, he continued on toward the theme park, almost desperate for Wednesday to arrive.

AND WEDNESDAY DID ARRIVE. Jeri came walking down the road at lunchtime, and she waved to him. "I just need a few minutes," she said.

He stood, something plaguing him. "I just have a quick question," he asked. They'd texted a lot over the past couple of days, and she'd eaten his frozen pizza with him on Monday and the soup-from-a-bag last night.

"Did you get your new tie?" she asked, detouring across the front lawn. "I left it on your back door."

"I got it." It felt like he'd be able to take her into his arms. The action would be effortless, and he wanted to do it so badly. He didn't. "I just thought of something we haven't talked about." He cleared his throat and looked toward the other cabins on the other side of Jeri's.

"What?" she asked.

"When we go to get...today, we're going to have to, you know, kiss."

Only the breeze whispered between them, and then Jeri started to laugh. "And you can't even look at me."

He focused on her, smiling at her when he found that sexy grin on her face. "I'm just saying it's something we haven't planned for."

"You'd like to practice, is that it?"

Yes. "Well, I'm not sure our first kiss should be as man and wife."

"You say that like there will be a second kiss." She twirled the ends of a lock of hair, clearly flirting with him.

He had to do something to show her he wanted to help her—and that he liked her. So he leaned closer, watching her intently so he didn't miss anything. He didn't touch her, but when he whispered, "A man can dream, right Jeri?" he saw the desire in her eyes. He backed up. One step, and then two. "I'm ready when you're ready."

Chapter Seven

J eri kept Sawyer waiting outside, her nerves inside the privacy of her cabin nearly drowning her.

"What am I doing?" she asked herself. And why in the world had Sawyer agreed to it?

For the good of the ranch, she thought, and she seized onto it. It would just be a few months, and then her license would be final, and she'd be able to finish the job here and set up shop somewhere else.

She'd never be able to stay here, not after this sham with a man she actually liked.

"And you're going to need an explanation for Scarlett," she said aloud to herself. She and Sawyer had talked every detail to death—except for a few, obviously.

She'd been dreaming of kissing him for a few nights now, and yet somehow, it had never crossed her mind that she'd have to kiss him in front of a judge. Or a city official.

Someone who'd sign the marriage certificate, at the very least.

Maybe they *should* practice.

"Jeri," Sawyer called from the front porch. "We're going to be late. I just checked the traffic, and—"

She pulled open the door, effectively silencing him. "I'm ready," she said. She'd laid out her dress that morning, and she could do her makeup in the truck. She never wore much anyway. She couldn't tame her curls, so she figured she'd just pull them up and wrap them into a knot on top of her head. Get them out of the way.

Get this whole marriage out of the way.

Intellectually, she knew she was kidding herself. Severely.

She'd seen the heat in Sawyer's eyes outside just now. Felt it burn way down in her gut. If she and Sawyer were going to get married, they'd definitely still see each other.

Of course we'll see each other, she thought. *We live next door to each other.*

But she knew there was another definition for "see" and it was akin to "dating."

And kissing. And hand-holding. And happiness.

And a huge risk.

"So are we going?" he asked, hooking his thumb over his shoulder. "Want me to grab your clothes?"

"They're right there," she said, indicating the garment bag draped over the back of the couch.

He stepped into her personal space, and Jeri should've

backed up. She should've just admitted to Scarlett she didn't have her license. Should've packed her bags and disappeared into the night, the way self-respecting women did.

Instead, she touched his arm. A feather-light touch that still got him to pause and look at her. "I want—" She started, but she had no idea how to finish. Her pulse pounded in the vein in her neck, and she might regret what she wanted.

She reached up and swept his cowboy hat off his head, trailing her fingers over his short hair and down the side of his face. Stretching up halfway, she really wanted him to come the rest of the way to kiss her.

He did, and Jeri pulled in a breath that was made of part shock and part relief. No matter what he said about how long he hadn't had a girlfriend, the man hadn't forgotten how to kiss. His lips tasted like mint, and she enjoyed the sensation of his hands along her waist and back as her fingers ran through his hair and across his shoulders.

He broke their kiss for less than a second, wherein he sucked in a breath, and then matched his lips to hers again.

Jeri sure hoped there would be more kissing after they got married. Maybe she could risk her heart for a man like Sawyer.

Sawyer pulled away again, his hands somehow cradling her face now. "Yeah," he said. "I think that was some good practice."

She giggled and tucked herself right into his arms, right where she belonged in that moment.

"We really are going to be late," he whispered, and she straightened.

"Let's do this." She moved in front of him and marched confidently down the steps and to his truck. He tossed her dress—the dress she was going to wear to marry him—in the back of the truck and got behind the wheel.

She slid over to sit beside him, tucking her hand in his after he adjusted the air conditioner. "I think we might have to tell Scarlett about the wedding."

"What? Why would we do that?"

"I'm going to have to give her a license with the last name of Smith on it. She's not stupid."

"Smith is a really common last name."

"We should decide what we're going to do if someone asks."

Sawyer waited until he'd driven off the ranch and past the robot before he spoke again. "Okay, look. My faith is important to me. I feel right about this, because you're not doing anything illegal to get your contractor's license. I've seen you work and your product, and you're good." He rumbled down the road, several seconds passing in silence.

"And we're both consenting adults. We're allowed to get married."

Jeri thought about that bone-melting kiss. They were definitely consenting adults.

"If someone asks what happened," Sawyer said. "I'm not sure I can lie to them."

"Just say we got married," Jeri said. "That'll be the truth."

"And we kept separate cabins next door to each other?" He shook his head. "I think we should loop Hudson and Scarlett in on this as soon as possible." He sighed and checked both ways for traffic before turning.

Jeri's mind spun. "We've been over all of this." Her thumbs were tired from all the texting.

"Yeah, I know," Sawyer said. "I'm just thinking out loud."

He did that a lot, Jeri knew. Their time together in the evenings, though they'd just had a couple, had proven that.

"Maybe we should talk to them. Let them know. Move in together." He looked at her, but Jeri could barely breathe.

"Move in together?" Her first instinct was to shake her head and call off the wedding. She could find another solution to the problem.

"My cabin has two bedrooms," Sawyer said.

"No," Jeri said. "No, we don't need to move in together." Maybe she could just give the paperwork to Scarlett and say it was her legal name, but she went by her maiden name because she'd never gotten around to changing it after the divorce.

Of course, that would require her to tell the story about Howie, but it was better than telling her *and* Hudson that she and Sawyer had agreed to a marriage of convenience. She explained her new plan to Sawyer, who continued to drive in silence for a few minutes.

"I can't find an argument for that," he said.

"I'm not asking you to lie," Jeri said.

"Good," Sawyer practically barked. "Because I'm not going to."

"I'm not going to either."

"Except about the last name."

Her jaw clenched, and she looked away. Technically, it would be a lie. A little, white lie that wouldn't hurt anyone, and in fact, would help a lot of people.

Sawyer slowed and pulled into a parking lot. "I'm sorry," he said. "I just...I don't quite know how to navigate this."

"I don't either. Believe it or not, I've never been fake-married before." He looked at her for a moment too long, and Jeri didn't like it. "What?" she asked.

"You said your last marriage was 'kind of' done because of a joke."

Foolishness hit Jeri, and not for the first time over that silly marriage. "This is a mistake."

"No," Sawyer said, putting his hand on her arm. "I didn't say that. I'm just saying, maybe...."

She waited, her emotions storming all over the place.

"Let's go," he said. "We're supposed to be here an hour early, and we're literally about to be late." He got out of the truck, collected their bags from the back while she slid out behind him, and took her hand in his as they walked toward the entrance.

"What were you going to say?" she asked.

"I'll tell you later," he said. "Do you have the marriage license?"

"Yes, right here." She lifted the folder she carried, her own anxiety doubling and then tripling before they went inside. It was cool, and it smelled like grapefruit and soap, and Jeri's emotions calmed.

Sawyer handled everything, from checking in with the clerk to passing over the marriage license. He followed the woman to the dressing room and handed Jeri her garment bag. She went into the dressing room to change, and this was not how Jeri had pictured ever getting married.

Of course, her first wedding hadn't fulfilled any little girl's dreams either. *And look how that turned out*, she thought as she stepped out of her jeans and into the simple, white dress she'd bought at the department store only two days ago.

She sniffled, wishing this wasn't what she was doing right now. And yet, she did it. Put on the dress. Zipped it up herself by some miracle. Put on the strappy shoes and looped gold hoops through her ears.

She hadn't done her makeup in the truck, so she took ten minutes to swipe on some mascara, make perfect points on her eyeliner, and put on a classic red lipstick that every bride should wear to tie the knot.

Someone knocked on one of the interior doors, and she went to open it, only to see Sawyer standing there.

"Cowboy hat or no cowboy hat?" he asked, reaching for it. "Off." He took it off and grinned. "Or on."

"On." She grinned at him. He really was wonderful, and she stepped into his arms. "Thank you," she whispered. "Thank you so much." He smelled like fresh air and pine trees, and she wanted to inhale him right into her soul.

"I think they're ready for us if you're ready," he said, stepping back. He held onto both of her hands and surveyed her. "You're beautiful."

"You're just saying that."

"I don't just say things," Sawyer said. "That's probably something you need to know before we get married."

There were dozens of things she needed to know before she married anyone for real, but that wasn't what was happening here.

"Noted," she said, painting that smile in place and choosing to look at this as a glass-half-full situation. "You look handsome too."

He wore a dark navy suit, a white shirt, and the tie she'd bought for him in town. It was purple and pink with gold paisleys stitched into it. He was the picture of cowboy groom perfection, and she couldn't believe he was going along with this favor.

"It's just a couple of months," she said, looking up and into his eyes.

"For the ranch," he said.

"For the ranch," she echoed.

He smiled, took her hand, and led her into the room where the ceremony would be held. They didn't have witnesses, so a couple of employees came in while the justice of the peace said a few words about love and marriage.

By the time Jeri said, "I do," and Sawyer said it back to her, she was ready to get out of the dress. Out of Van Nuys. Away from everything.

"You may kiss your bride," the man who'd just married them said, and Sawyer turned toward her with a wide smile on his face.

And when she kissed him this time, it was just as magical and just as beautiful as that first kiss on her porch only a couple of hours ago.

So maybe not *every*thing was fake about this marriage. Jeri honestly wasn't sure, and the lines were starting to blur already. What she did know was that she wanted to keep kissing Sawyer.

So she did that.

Chapter Eight

Sawyer hadn't spent a whole lot of time imagining his wedding day or what it would be like. His family would've been there at the very least, not a secretary as a witness, and not a justice of the peace instead of a pastor.

But kissing Jeri…that about made up for the other shortcomings this wedding had.

She pulled away first, a smile on her face, and the weak applause ceased. Sawyer looked at the four other people in the room, and said, "All right. I guess that's it."

And that was that. He was married to Jeri Bell.

Just for a few months.

For the ranch.

He thought of Gramps, and how much the ranch meant to the old man. Scarlett had come in, and Sawyer had been worried at first. But he shouldn't have been. She had her grandmother's spirit, and she dug in with everything she had, cleaning things up and securing funding the animals on the ranch desperately needed.

And Jeri was providing the housing they needed. Sawyer admired them all, and he once again felt peace speaking to his heart.

"See you out there?" Jeri asked, and he nodded, turning away to go back into the men's locker room. He wasn't going to change back into his street clothes. Not yet. They'd get their paperwork, go file for Jeri's general contractor license, and then they were going to dinner.

Once alone, Sawyer's head spun. He couldn't believe he'd woken up single this morning and he was married now. It felt like this day had happened to another man. And he was supposed to just keep living his life on the ranch like normal.

He wasn't sure he could, because everything had changed. Hadn't it?

Just the fact that Jeri kissed him like she wanted to had changed everything.

He pushed the thoughts away. They were simply a rotating door anyway, going round and round and never getting anywhere.

He made it out to the lobby first, though he wasn't sure what Jeri was doing. She didn't talk to her family all that often, so she wouldn't be catching her mother up on her latest relationship status. She hadn't spoken of any friends from her past, except to say her foreman had betrayed her and she'd lost her entire crew and company.

Sorrow pulled through him, but he put a smile on his face as he stepped over to the counter to get their official paperwork. Jeri would need it for the license application, and he'd just taken it from the secretary when she came out.

With her hair all swooped up like that, and her makeup adding to her beauty, Sawyer's breath caught.

"You two are so cute," the secretary said. "Thanks for letting me stand in as a witness today. I can tell you're going to make it." She finished speaking just as Jeri arrived at his side.

Sawyer had no clue what to say.

"Thank you so much," Jeri said, linking her arm through his. "You ready, cowboy?"

Cowboy.

How had he never known she was such a flirt before? And wow, he liked the endearment aimed at him, in her voice.

"Where are you going for your honeymoon?" the woman asked, and Sawyer's whole body filled with flames.

"Oh, we can't take time off," Jeri said, and she sounded so natural. "So we're just celebrating tonight, and then we'll be back at work tomorrow."

"Oh, that's too bad," the secretary said.

"Yeah." Jeri smiled sunbeams at her, and Sawyer decided it was time to go.

"Ready," he said, tipping his hat at the secretary and turning away. Jeri held onto him all the way out of the building—and all the way to the truck. He loaded up their bags and put his arms around Jeri again, right there in the parking lot.

Maybe he didn't know everything about her. Yet.

Maybe they weren't going to celebrate their marriage tonight with more than chips and salsa. This time. Maybe they couldn't go on a honeymoon. Right now.

His thoughts surprised him, as did the way Jeri melted effortlessly into him. The slide of her fingers across the back of his neck sent desire coursing through him, and he wisely stepped away.

"Let's go get your license," he said, making one more attempt to focus on the real reason they'd just said I do.

By NIGHTFALL, he passed the mailbox robot that stood guard at the entrance to Last Chance Ranch. Jeri had fallen asleep on the way back from Santa Monica, where they'd wandered the pier, ridden the Ferris wheel, walked along the beach, and then eaten dinner.

"We're back," he said, trying to find the right pet name for her. Nothing came, and he fell silent again.

She sat up from where she'd been leaning into him, a yawn coming from her mouth. "Sorry I fell asleep."

"It's fine," he said. "There was a lot of traffic. Took forever."

"Howie wanted someone to talk to while we sat in traffic," she said, and it may have been one of the rare times Jeri didn't have her sunshiney persona hitched perfectly in place. He loved how optimistic and vibrant she was. But it was nice to see she had another side to her. One that thought through things and could have a real conversation.

"Well," Sawyer said. "I'm not Howie."

"No, you're not." Jeri looked at him, and in the near darkness, the lines of her face were soft and she looked sleepy and sexy at the same time.

His heart beat kicked into the next gear, and he looked away to pull into his driveway. Blue came trotting down the front steps, and Sawyer was glad he'd at least have his dog for company that night.

He and Jeri moved like thieves in the night, as he carried her bag back to her cabin and followed her up the steps. She hadn't locked her front door, and she went into the darkness first, snapping on a lamp in the next moment.

He followed her, almost desperate to kiss her again. Tell her how he really felt. After laying the bag over the back of the couch where it had been earlier, he went into the kitchen, where she stood in front of the fridge.

"Something to drink?" she asked him. "I have water or...water."

"Water's fine," he said, though he wasn't thirsty and he had water at his own house next door.

She handed him a bottle and he twisted the cap off anyway. "Okay." She blew out her breath. "So now what?"

Surprise shot through Sawyer. "We've already talked about now what," he said.

She cocked one eyebrow at him, which made him smile. Maybe he was simply too tired for serious conversations right now. He had been up later than usual the past few nights as they texted out plans and details. As he laid in bed and thought about his sexy next-door neighbor he had real feelings for.

"I think a few things have changed," Jeri said, her dark eyes like pools of midnight in this dim lighting.

He chuckled, and it sounded darker than he liked. "Oh, some things have changed," he agreed.

She took a long drink of her water and glanced around the cabin like she might find other people there, listening.

Sawyer felt like he might be sick, but he had to say something. "Look, Jeri, I just have to say one thing." He waited until her gaze settled on him again, which somehow made talking harder. "I like you."

Three little words.

"Like, for real. Not just for a couple of months. Not just for the ranch." Was that plain enough for her?

"I like you too," she said. "We're friends."

Frustration combined with anger in Sawyer's gut, and he hadn't felt that way since leaving the racing circuit. "No." He set his untouched bottle of water on the counter behind him. "Not just friends."

Friends didn't kiss each other the way she kissed him. And he'd been careful not to pour too much emotion into his kiss, but he knew he had. Passion and desire swam between them whenever they touched. She had to feel it too.

Before she could deny him again, he swept his arm around her waist and pulled her closer. A hint of shock moved through her expression.

"Not just friends," he repeated, lowering his mouth to hers. Maybe he'd read her wrong. Maybe in the heat of the moment, she'd somehow conveyed something she hadn't meant to.

But all of that was over now. She couldn't be nervous about going to get married, or worried about making sure the justice of the peace believed they were in love.

Right now, in this cabin, it was just the two of them, and they didn't need to hide.

And she didn't.

She kissed him with that same slow precision she had earlier. The flames in his belly licked upward as the kiss lengthened and deepened. Finally satisfied, he pulled away, glad when she stayed within the circle of his arms and leaned her head against his chest.

He stayed in that moment for as long as he could. Then he realized his brain was screaming at him to get on home now.

"I'll see you in the morning," he whispered, stepping delicately out of her arms and heading for the front door. To his great credit, he didn't look back.

Inside his own cabin, his pulse and his breathing labored through him as if he'd just run a marathon and not walked thirty yards across the grass.

Blue nudged his hand, and that set Sawyer into motion.

"Yeah, let's see if you have dinner," he said to the dog. He turned on lights in the cabin and filled up his dog's food and water bowls.

Normal things. Common stuff.

Brushing his teeth and putting away the suit he'd been married in that day. Saying a prayer and climbing into bed. He looked at the empty space next to him and tried to envision Jeri there with him.

She fit.

Maybe he didn't know everything about her. But he wanted to, and he was going to perpetuate their relationship. With those hopeful thoughts in his head, he finally fell asleep with a smile on his face.

THE NEXT MORNING, he rose with the dawn, as usual. "Another day in paradise," he muttered to himself as he made coffee and padded down the hall to shower. He sometimes bathed two or three times a day, depending on that day's work. Today, he'd be in the stables, where he'd surely see Hudson at some point.

Hudson wasn't his boss. He didn't have to tell the man anything. But they'd become friends over the past several months, and a knuckle of unrest entered his mind as he set his cowboy hat on his head, filled his coffee mug, and went out to the front porch with Blue.

Their morning routine hadn't changed just because he'd gotten married yesterday. Maybe nothing else would either.

"Except for the fact that you can kiss Jeri Bell now," he said to himself, looking toward her cabin. Her chickens clucked happily, and dang if the noise didn't make him smile.

She came out the back door like she usually did. Spoke to her chickens as normal. He'd never heard what she said to them, only the timbre of her voice as it lifted into the silence of the ranch. If she followed her normal routine, she'd be leaving for work soon, and he'd get to see her.

He took another sip of his coffee, the liquid breakfast he always had first almost gone. How he loved black coffee—something he should probably tell his wife.

His *wife.*

Right on schedule, the woman came around from the back of her house, walking between their two cabins. Would she come say hello at least? He hoped for a kiss, but he knew she wouldn't be that bold. After all, Hudson, Carson, Dave, or Cache could come walking out of their cabins at any moment.

"Morning, Sawyer," she said, lifting her hand in a wave. That sunny smile sat on her face, and Sawyer drank it all up.

"Morning, Jeri," he called back, gladness seeping through him. She continued on her way down the road, and Sawyer watched her until she turned the corner and disappeared. Normal. That was normal.

"Hey," Dave said, startling Sawyer away from his thoughts.

"Yeah, morning, Dave," he said, standing up. "What's going on?"

"Cache needs some help with the cattle this morning. Two coyotes came onto the ranch last night, and we've been tasked to ensure all the animals have somewhere safe to sleep at night." Dave took off his cowboy hat, swept his hair back, and sighed. "We're starting with the cattle, and moving from there."

"All right," Sawyer said, suddenly glad it would be a very busy day at Last Chance Ranch. Then he wouldn't be able to think so hard about Jeri.

Chapter Nine

Jeri went straight to the homestead to give Scarlett her new application, Sawyer's typical morning greeting looping through her mind. She'd prepared a speech about the new last name, so grateful Sawyer had a common name that thousands of other people did.

But Scarlett didn't even look at it. She was in a frenzy about a couple of coyotes that had arrived at the ranch and broken a couple of fences. The folder with the paperwork got set on the counter, and she turned right back to Hudson, who had a large map spread across the dining room table.

"What's going on?" Jeri asked, taking in the man's worried face. He'd disappeared from the ranch last month after he and Scarlett had broken up. But he was back now, and they were back together and more in love than ever.

Jeri might have been jealous before.

"Coyotes," Hudson said. "We're strengthening all the

fences today. Making sure all the barns can lock up tight. No garbage is to be left out."

"Can you help today?" Scarlett asked, her face full of worry. "I don't want to lose chickens to the coyotes."

"I'm surprised they didn't take Feathers or Spot," Jeri said, her stomach tightening at the thought of losing her pets. "They don't even have a coop."

"There were only two of them," Hudson said. "Cache spotted them late last night as he was on his way home."

"Which is still highly suspicious," Scarlett said. "I mean, why was he out at almost midnight, just walking around?"

"Sometimes a man needs an open sky to think," Hudson said, his voice soft and thoughtful as he studied the map. "If Dave, Cache, and Sawyer can get the cattle contained, then they can move onto the llamas, the pigs, and the horses."

"Okay," Scarlett said. "I can work with Amber, Karla, and Sissy to make sure the dogs, cats, and goats are secure."

"That leaves the chickens," Hudson said. "They usually just wander at night."

"I can build them a coop," Jeri said. "We can fence it and make sure they're inside before nightfall."

Scarlett looked at her. "You can build a coop in one day?"

"If I have to," Jeri said. "I started a small one at my place for my chickens. But maybe once you guys are done doing all you need to, you can send me some help. We'll get it done." She glanced at Hudson and back to Scarlett. "I'm surprised there's not a chicken land here already."

"Well," Scarlett said with a giant smile. "It wouldn't be chicken land. Maybe something like Chicken...Country."

"Country fried chicken," Hudson said, and Scarlett swatted him on the chest.

"No," she said, laughing. "Chicken clan."

"Chicken clique," Hudson suggested.

"No, no," Scarlett said. "It has to have the ch-sound. Chicken...Church?"

"Church?" Hudson asked. "You can't be serious."

Jeri basked in the playfulness between them. "I've got it," she said, "Poultry...Pack."

"Party," Scarlett said. "Poultry Party."

"Land," Hudson added. "Poultry Partyland."

"We have a winner," Scarlett announced, and Hudson swept his arm around her as they laughed together. Jeri joined in, because their joy was infectious, and she liked laughing.

They sobered, and Scarlett said, "Okay, so let's get this done."

Jeri nodded and stepped over to the map. So she wouldn't be working in the dog enclosure today. It didn't matter. She wasn't racing against the clock anymore, desperate to show Scarlett and Jewel that she was the best general contractor in the state, even if she didn't have a license.

"So where do we want Poultry Partyland?" she asked.

"There's land out here." Hudson pointed to the area south of the homestead.

"No, Karla's got something in mind for that," Scarlett said, causing Hudson to lift his eyebrows. "Something for tourists. We'll talk about it later." She glanced at Jeri. "It would mean a lot more construction, and we've already got a lot going on right now."

Jeri's heart took courage at the mention of more construction. She'd get the job if she bid on it, which of course, she would. "What about here?" She indicated a stretch of land bordering Horse Heaven she knew didn't have anything on it. "There are stables and stalls there already. The chicken coop would fit there—how many chickens are we talking?"

Scarlett's face went into concentration mode. "They're hard to count," she said. "They just wander."

"Enough for thirty or forty, wouldn't you say?" Hudson asked.

"Yeah," Scarlett agreed. "That should be fine." They both looked at Jeri. "Can we do that?"

"Absolutely," she said. "I have lumber at the dog enclosure. I'll get started right away."

"I'll send someone over as soon as I can," Scarlett said.

"No problem," Jeri said, though she'd never been an entire chicken coop in a single day, by herself. Construction was generally much slower than that. But there were coyotes at play, and she thought of her beloved Feathers and Spot, and she'd get the coop done. They needed somewhere to sleep too, and while she loved her pets, she didn't want two chickens in the house with her.

As she went over to the dog enclosure to get lumber, she pulled out her phone to text Sawyer. *She didn't even look at the paperwork. I think we're in the clear.*

He didn't respond right away, and Jeri stuffed her phone in her pocket and focused on her job. She'd fought hard to be here. Done crazy things. She wasn't going to blow her chance to rebuild her life because she couldn't stop thinking about a certain pair of dreamy hazel eyes and a kiss that had changed her life.

BY LUNCHTIME, Jeri had some serious reservations about being able to finish the coop on time. She'd used the wall of the existing stables, which had sped things up considerably. But the ground was soft, and she was having a hard time getting it ready to build on.

She'd gone over it several times with the roller vehicle, and it was finally time to put in the supports. She'd build the nesting boxes and framework for the roosts, but the coop needed walls. And she couldn't put in walls if the ground wouldn't hold them up.

"We really need to pour concrete," she told herself, but there wasn't time for concrete right now. But she could do quick-crete, just in the holes for the main supports. That meant another trip over to the dog's construction site. More hauling of equipment and tools.

She'd just arrived back at the coop site with everything

she needed to find Cache and Sawyer standing there admiring her roosts and nesting boxes.

"Hey, boys," she said as she got out of her work truck. "What's up?"

"We've been sent to help," Cache said. "We got the cattle contained and ready for tonight."

"Great," Jeri said, lowering the tailgate. She explained the situation with the ground and directed them to get the quick-crete bags and help her get the main supports set. Once again, concrete would make the best surface for the coop, and she wondered if they had enough to do the floor too.

"Help me figure this out," she said. "Do I have enough quick-crete to do the floor? It sure would make cleaning the coop easier." She pulled the notebook where she'd sketched the coop closer and started writing numbers on it.

"I think I need four more bags," she said.

"I can run to town," Cache said. "We need chicken wire too, right?"

"Yeah," Jeri said, scraping her hair off her forehead. Why was it so hot in September? "Could you? That would be great."

"I'll go now," he said, and Jeri told him the keys were still in the ignition. He climbed behind the wheel of her truck, leaving her alone with Sawyer.

"We can at least build the frame for the coop and the run," she said. "Get them set with what we have."

"All right," he said. "Boss me." Sawyer didn't act

strange at all, but there was a new energy flowing between them as they worked together. He could do almost anything, and she gave him instructions and he got the job done.

"How'd you sleep?" he asked, and that was new.

"Okay," she admitted, glancing at him. "You?"

"Oh, I laid awake forever." He shot her a glance filled with flirtatious heat. "Thinking about my wife." Grinning, he turned and nailed the top of the run to the post they'd set.

Jeri glanced around to see if anyone had approached. They were in the clear. "Yeah, well, maybe we should eat together again tonight."

"That's not a maybe," he said.

A smile filled her soul, but she kept it off her face. "I suppose you're cooking then? I haven't had time to get groceries, and I'm pretty sure all I have is water."

He laughed, working deftly as he did. "I can find something. Or we could go to town."

"I think we're going to be working here for a while," she said. "Let's not plan on having time to go to town." Plus, she was exhausted already. This week had been one of emotional highs and so much planning and worrying. She felt like she needed another weekend at the beach to recover, but on a ranch, there was work to be done seven days a week. If Sawyer left for a family picnic, someone else picked up his chores.

"Hold it steady there," she said, wishing she had a third arm she could use to check for the height of both ends of the run. But she'd already measured. Dug the holes right. Filled them in.

She let go of her post and bent to secure it with the quick-crete. This fast-drying concrete worked in a pinch, and it was surprisingly durable. Especially in California, where the weather wasn't as severe as say, somewhere like Denver or Salt Lake.

"Got this one," she said, moving toward Sawyer. He held the post, his biceps tight. He was strong, and beautiful, and Jeri lost her focus for a few seconds as she admired him. Then she bent and made sure the post was properly grounded and the concrete all in the hole. She smoothed it and said, "Done."

He let go and stepped back. "Yeah, that looks good." They finished the other two posts, and then all she needed to do for the outside run was staple chicken wire all around it.

"You wanna come hold the gate for me while I put on the hinges?" She smiled at Sawyer, working with him much more fun now than it had been last week.

"Yep." He followed her, the scent of his cologne and sweat making her light-headed. They worked well together, and she enjoyed his company.

"It's so hot," she complained.

"Yeah," he said. "Some people say you get used to it, but I've lived my whole life in California, and I think they're lying."

She laughed as she fitted the hinge into the holes she'd drilled. "Yeah, I've lived here my whole life too."

"Yeah?" he asked.

"Yeah," she said. "Went to school at Cal Poly. Got my construction management degree."

"That's great," he said. "I love San Luis Obispo."

"Me too." She beamed at him. "I started my business there." Ended it too, but she'd already told him most of that story.

"Where do you think you'll settle next?" he asked.

Her eyes flew to his. "What do you mean?"

"I mean, you can't live at Last Chance Ranch forever. You're starting over, right?" His smile had fled, and his eyes harbored a seriousness she'd appreciated in the past.

"Yeah," she said slowly.

"So you'll rebuild your contracting business somewhere." There was a question in there, he just hadn't used any of the usual phrases.

"Yes," she said, finishing the bottom hinge partway and moving to the top. That way, she could get them both in and balanced before tightening them all the way. Her mind continued to work as quickly as her fingers did. Thankfully, she'd done thousands of hinges over the years, and she didn't have to think too hard about that work.

"So it's a secret," Sawyer finally said, breaking the silence between them. Jeri finished with the bottom hinge, and gave the middle one a last tightening too.

She straightened and looked at Sawyer. "It's not a secret. I simply don't know."

"Haven't thought that far ahead."

"Until yesterday," she said. "I thought I'd never have the opportunity to even think about rebuilding my business." She handed him the screwdriver she'd been using and swung the gate closed to test it. "And this morning, we woke up to coyotes. So no. I haven't thought that far ahead."

She started to walk away, unsure of why his questions and insinuations that she should've been forward-thinking bothered her. But they did.

"Hey," he said, catching her hand in his. "I didn't mean to upset you."

Every cell softened with his touch. "You didn't," she said, only half the truth. "I just...." She sighed and gazed at the pastures of wild grass between here and the homestead. "I just hadn't thought that my time on this ranch was limited. But you're right. It is."

Which meant her time with *him* was limited.

But of course, she already knew that. *Just for a couple of months.*

Her project would keep her here until February—and then what? She wasn't sure, but she had six months to figure it out. In a couple of months, she could start looking at upcoming jobs and put in bids on them. She knew the game. She knew how to play it.

The real question was, did she even want to?

Sawyer squeezed her hand. "What are you thinking?"

"I'm thinking I've been living day by day since the accident. Just making it through." And that did upset her. "I'm thinking I need a plan for my life, now that I know I can actually rebuild it."

"Not everything has to be planned," he said. "Life doesn't really have a blueprint."

"No?" She looked at him, finding comfort in those pond-colored eyes. "You didn't have a plan when you quit the family business?"

"No," he said quietly. "I didn't. I knew it needed to be done, and I did it. It's a lot like how I came to the decision to marry you."

"You knew it needed to be done, and you did it." She shook her head, so many emotions coiling through her. "I don't know if I should be grateful or offended."

"Why would you be offended?"

She almost slammed her toolbox shut, but she still needed it open so she just tossed the screwdriver on top. "Because you've been kissing me like it means something." A storm gathered in her chest. "But now you're saying it was just something you knew you needed to do, like cleaning out a stall or something. So which is it?"

Sawyer blinked at her, his eyes wide. "That's not what I meant."

Jeri cocked her hip as if preparing for battle. "What did you mean, then?"

Chapter Ten

S awyer couldn't find the right words to explain, at least about his decision to marry her. "I came to Last Chance Ranch several years ago," he said, wishing she'd take the challenge out of her expression. "Gramps was here, of course. His wife hadn't died yet either." Sawyer grew a little somber, and Jeri relaxed slightly.

He took her other hand in his so he was holding both. "They were so cute together. She was so sick, and yet she'd go out to take care of the cats every day." He smiled and shook his head at the memories flowing through him.

"I didn't have a plan to come here, not at first. I knew I wasn't supposed to be working for my father anymore, and I knew I loved animals. I actually thought I'd be able to buy a ranch of my own, but that didn't pan out." He thought back to that time, realizing now that those trying months had changed him.

"There were a few very hard months," he said quietly, the wide sky above them almost stealing his words away from him. "But eventually, I came north, and I met Gramps at the grocery store where he was hanging a sign for help on this ranch. I followed him up, and I've been here ever since."

Jeri gave him a small smile, one without showing her pretty teeth. "That's a nice story."

He heard the undercurrent in her voice. *But it doesn't tell me why you decided to marry me.*

"I prayed about it," he said. "Everything felt right. So I just...leapt."

"And that's what you did with me," she filled in, still an acidic bite to her words.

"I suppose," he said, the need to defend himself boiling up inside his chest. "And I'm not playing with you, Jeri. I might remind you that you kissed me first." He grinned at her. "I know we don't know each other real well yet, but you'll find that I don't do or say much that I don't absolutely mean."

She studied his face for a moment, and then she nodded. "All right. I can accept that."

"Good," Sawyer said, glancing around. "So, what else can we do while we wait for Cache to show up with that concrete?"

THE FOLLOWING WEEK, Sawyer didn't sit on his front steps sipping coffee like he usually did. Today, Carson was leaving Last Chance Ranch to try his hand at dairy farming in Texas. Adele, his girlfriend, had left for New York City already, and he couldn't stand to stay in California without her.

Sawyer took Blue over to say good-bye to Carson's dogs while he helped the cowboy load up everything he'd brought from his ranch in Montana.

"I sure hate to see you go," Sawyer said, wondering if he'd be able to stay in his cabin once Jeri moved out of hers.

"I know," Carson said, and nothing else. Sawyer had never been in love. Not the kind of love that drove a man to pack up everything he owned and drive away because the memories were too hard to deal with.

Sawyer picked up two more boxes and went outside. He wanted to tell someone about him and Jeri, and Carson was leaving the ranch. He was an outgoing guy and had fit in with everyone on the ranch almost immediately—except Adele. They'd fought like cats and dogs at first, and then they'd fallen in love.

So Sawyer's relationship with Jeri was less volatile. Calmer. Secret.

He liked secret, and he decided to keep his marriage to the curvy brunette to himself. When they were almost finished packing, Hudson and Scarlett showed up. Scarlett had obviously been crying already, and she hugged Carson tightly.

"You can stay," she said. "We need you here."

"I can't stay," Carson said, stepping back.

She wiped her eyes and nodded. "When Adele gets back, you should be here."

"She's not coming back," Carson said quietly. He glanced at Hudson, who put his arm around Scarlett.

"Let the man go," he said, shaking Carson's hand.

"Okay." Scarlett sniffed. "But I just know she's going to realize what a big mistake she made and come back to you."

"Well, she can find me at Shiloh Ridge in Texas," Carson said, lifting his chin. Sawyer admired him. He'd lost his ranch in Montana, and now his girlfriend had chosen her culinary career over him.

The trials other people went through reminded Sawyer that he could do hard things too. Weather any storm. He shook Carson's hand too, and said, "We're going to miss you around here."

"That's just because you'll have to pick up my chores until Scarlett hires someone," he joked, and Sawyer laughed with him.

"I've already got someone," Scarlett said. "His name is Lance Longcomb, and he'll be here next week."

"Still have double chores for a week," Sawyer said, a smile on his face. "It's fine, Scarlett," he added when her face crumpled again. "Boy, that's not what I meant." He looked at Hudson for help, and he nodded at Sawyer.

"She's fine. She's just feeling like part of the family is leaving. And with Adele...." He trailed off, turned Scarlett away from Sawyer and Carson, and took her back to his cabin.

"She's great," Carson said as they watched her go.

"She is," Sawyer said, catching sight of Jeri as she emerged from her back yard. She glanced to his porch and paused. It felt real nice to know she was looking for him, and heat warmed his feet, moving up through his entire body.

"Well, I suppose I better get started on your chores," Sawyer said, and he shook Carson's hand again.

"Thanks for everything," he said, and Sawyer nodded.

"Let me know how Shiloh Ridge is," he said. "Maybe I'll follow you out there."

Carson cocked his head and looked at Sawyer with curiosity in his eyes. In the end, he said nothing. Just nodded and got behind the wheel of his truck. Sawyer watched him rumble down the road, off on a new adventure in a new place.

For a while there, after he'd quit training horses, Sawyer had thought he wanted an adventure too. But he hadn't. He'd met Gramps and come to this ranch, and it had been his home ever since.

He started down the road to his house, calling, "Jeri," after her as she proceeded down the lane.

She turned, and Sawyer's heart did backflips. "Hey," he said, jogging up to her.

"You weren't on the porch."

"I was helping Carson get packed up. He left today."

"Oh, that's right." She looked to her left as if she'd still be able to see his truck. The dust still hung in the morning air, but the truck and the man were gone. "It was weird, not seeing you there. You're so routined."

"You say that like it's a bad thing." He took her hand and they started walking together toward the road that led further into the ranch.

"I didn't mean it like that," she said. "I was worried. For as long as I've been here, you sip your coffee on the front steps." She flinched, nearly jumping into his arms. Then her laughter filled the air. "Oh, hey, Blue. You scared me." She paused to crouch down and scrub his dog behind the ears. "Your nose is wet. Did you know that? Did you?"

Sawyer's soul felt alive as he watched them interact. Blue would take a good rub-down from anyone; he wasn't picky. Jeri clearly loved him, and the feeling was mutual. She straightened and asked, "What's on your schedule for today?"

He exhaled heavily. "Well, with Carson gone, I think I'm in the stables all morning. I'll take care of your chickens." He beamed at her. "And then I have to go help Cache with the cattle. And I'm sure the pigs will need something."

"They always do," she said with a giggle.

He dropped his gaze to her lips. He hadn't kissed her in a week, though they were still sharing dinner together every night. He did like his routines, and they had fallen into an easy one. He showered after a long day on the ranch, and she came over whenever she happened to finish her work for the day.

He had dinner waiting in the oven for them, and they ate together, talked about their day, the ranch, their previous lives, and she left to sleep in her own cabin. Sometimes they sat at the table to eat and talk. Sometimes on the couch. He liked that best, as she let him hold her hand afterward, and she cuddled into him like she needed him.

"You're staring at my mouth," Jeri said, and when he drew his attention back to her eyes, she had that one eyebrow cocked at him.

"Maybe I'm thinking about kissing you," he said, feeling bold and brave as every cell buzzed in his body. She made him feel things he'd never felt before. Made him realize he hadn't really been living before she showed up on the ranch.

"Maybe you should just do it," she said. "The staring is a little creepy."

He laughed, drawing her into an embrace that felt playful and fun, yet serious at the same time. "I sure like you, Jeri," he said, just before touching his lips to hers. It was a light kiss, a seeking permission kiss.

Jeri gave her permission, and kissed him back in a needful, passionate way that had him baking under the morning sun.

A horn sounded—a long, drawn-out blaring noise—that caused him to jump apart from Jeri. Across the grassy expanse, on the parallel road, the other side of the U-shaped Cabin Community, Hudson sat in his truck, the window rolled down.

He wore a huge smile on his face and he waved as if he

were a five-year-old seeing their grandmother for the first time in a while.

"Oh, boy," Sawyer said, watching the truck move forward and turn toward the homestead.

"Yeah," Jeri said, her phone chiming. She pulled it out of her back pocket and looked at it. "Scarlett wants me to come to the homestead for lunch." She sighed, the sound full of resignation. "She wants you to come too."

Chapter Eleven

Jeri just wanted to get to the homestead and confess everything to Scarlett right then. "Confess" wasn't the right word either. She didn't have to justify her relationship with Sawyer. As he'd said, they were both consenting adults. He'd signed his name; she'd signed hers. They'd both said I do.

Sawyer peered over her shoulder at the device still in her hand. "I don't care," he said, falling back a couple of steps. "You decide when you want to go and text me." He started walking back toward his house.

"Where are you going?" she called after him.

"Gotta do my morning ritual." He turned around and walked backward for a few steps, the smile on his face as bright as the sun. Okay, maybe not that bright. It was sweltering today, and September was supposed to bring cooler temperatures.

Jeri waved to him and returned her attention to her phone. She frowned and then tapped out, *I don't have time to come to the homestead at lunchtime.*

Not only did she not take a lunch, she really didn't have time for a conversation. She'd been behind since spending an entire day building a chicken coop last week. Dave had gone to town to buy some shower board to put under the roosts, and she was glad she didn't have the job of cleaning those off.

She started for the Canine Club, determined to do a day and a half's worth of work in a single day. If Scarlett wanted to talk to her, she knew where to find her—with a hammer in her hand and her tool belt around her waist.

Are you dating Sawyer? Scarlett's next text read.

"Something like that," she muttered, silencing her phone and shoving it in her pocket. She was extraordinarily skilled at doing multiple things at once, but walking and texting had never brought her anything but trouble. So she'd get to the building she was working on, and then she'd respond to her boss.

But she didn't know what to say once she got there. Was she dating Sawyer? She'd already married the man, and that step usually came after dating.

She figured a one-word answer would let Scarlett know that Jeri didn't really have time for texting either. Tapping out *yes*, she decided against it. After deleting it, she typed, *Did it look like we were dating?* and sent that instead.

She really couldn't leave her phone on silent while she

worked. She had suppliers calling her all the time, and she was expecting at least two phone calls that day—one from the electrician she'd contracted with and one from the HVAC company.

With the phone turned back up, she set it in her toolbox, its usual spot while she worked, and grabbed the sunscreen from the workbench. She may be a Californian born and bred, but even she'd burn if she didn't take some precautions.

She slicked clear chapstick over her lips, smacked them together, and said, "All right, boys. Let's build something." Dust flew into the air when she clapped her hands, and she imagined the other fifteen pairs that used to clap with her.

They didn't sound today, just like they hadn't for the past six months.

Jeri allowed herself the single moment of reflection, her face tipped toward heaven, and then she said, "Thank you for bringing me here." A deep breath later, she added, "Thank you for Sawyer Smith."

She didn't quite know how else to articulate how she felt about Sawyer. He'd asked her for a few hours with his family. She'd done something much more life-altering.

With a sense of calm and peace draping her, she picked up her plans and looked for the mark that indicated where she'd left off yesterday. "Gates," she said. She'd cut them all. Now all she needed to do was install them, put on the locks, and put up the square-holed fencing that allowed humans to see in and stay safe from the dogs. This enclosure was six-sided, with a space for three dogs to live in on each side.

So six gates. Six fencing installations. Then onto drywall.

She'd completed one dog enclosure identical to this, and it had taken her three-quarters of a day to get the gates and fencing done. She'd moved right onto drywall then, and she would again today.

"Today," she said, breathing out with the word. "We're going to get the gates and fencing done by lunch." She stretched her back and got to work, thinking it sure was easier to put on hinged doors when she had a pair of strong Sawyer-shaped hands to help her.

Maybe now that she had a real general contractor's license coming, she could start to build her business again. She knew what to do. How to file for business status. How to recruit the best carpenters. How to find the cheapest sub-contractors.

Her thoughts moved through the list of tasks she'd done before, and she determined to start that night. Almost everything could be done online these days, and she'd file for a small business in the state of California, and she'd start looking on the job boards to see what the going rate was for handymen this month.

Even if it wasn't Sawyer—and she certainly couldn't steal him away from ranch duties now that Carson was gone —Jeri did need some help. She'd talk to Scarlett about the funding from Forever Friends. They were paying for all the construction and her salary, she knew that.

"If you hire someone," she said to herself. "It'll come out of your money." Which was fine, honestly. Scarlett didn't make her pay rent, and living mortgage-free for the last couple of months had allowed her to put some of her lost savings back in the bank.

Her phone rang while she had the door braced with one hand and the electric screwdriver in the other. No way she could answer it. So she let it ring, driving the screws into the wood to keep the door hanging.

Finished, she grunted as she got up. Re-ponytailing her hair, she stepped over to the tool box to see who'd called. Turner's.

She dialed Philo back, and he picked up on the first ring. "I've got everything, and I'm on my way up," he said. "But I've somehow missed the turnoff to the ranch. Which road is it again?"

"Axel Bluff," she said. "Turn right off of Whitetail, and go straight up."

"That's right. Be there in a few."

Jeri hung up and turned back to the hexagonal shape, sighing. She'd done three gates, and it was eleven o'clock. She could take a break until Philo arrived, then she'd maybe be able to use him in a pinch while he worked on the HVAC system in the enclosure.

Philo never worked without a radio, and Scarlett looked forward to an afternoon of music and conversation she rarely got now that she worked alone. She wrestled with the fencing, getting it tacked and in position just as Philo pulled up, a steady bass beat coming from his van outside.

She usually went out to greet her subs, but if she stepped away from this fencing, she'd have to get it back in place all over again. The bass turned off, and a door slammed, and she called, "Philo, come help."

He entered the enclosure a few seconds later, jumping over with the words, "Hey, let me help."

"Thanks," she said, and she made quick work of nailing everything in place after that. "I definitely need a second pair of hands sometimes."

"You're doing this one alone too?" he asked, glancing around.

"Well, I've been busy," she said with a smile. "How the heck are you?"

"Great." He smiled at her the way she imagined her father would, though Philo wasn't nearly as old as her dad. In fact, he was probably only ten or fifteen years older than her.

"And Zelda?"

"Oh, she's puttering around in the garden almost all the time." Philo sighed. "Well, let's get this building some heat and AC, shall we?" He glanced around and moved over to the workbench in the middle of the space. "I can set up here?"

"Set on up there," she said. "And I want something from the eighties or later. None of your seventies crap."

He laughed and stepped out of the building. Jeri wiped her hand across her face and forehead, ready for the air conditioning Philo had promised. He whistled outside, but then suddenly stopped. He spoke to someone, but Jeri couldn't hear the words as she struggled with another piece of heavy fencing.

It was pretty clear though. Someone had come to visit her at the enclosure. She hoped it would be Sawyer, but ever since they'd gotten married, he didn't just stop by to chat.

Scarlett then.

Sure enough, the auburn-haired owner walked through the door a moment later. "Next time I come to visit, we'll have air conditioning." She looked absolutely gleeful about this, but she wasn't the one sweating buckets.

"Yes," Jeri said. "Can you come help?" If she was going to be here, she might as well hold up some fencing.

"Sure." Scarlett stepped over, looking behind her. "I wanted to have Karla meet with you."

"Oh?" Jeri asked as Karla came inside the enclosure too. She wore more professional clothes than was required for a working ranch with over one hundred and fifty animals. But she was the marketing director, so Jeri supposed that made sense. "Hey, Karla."

"Jeri, you're a genius."

"I have a blueprint," Jeri said. "It's not that hard."

"I can't even put together Legos," she said, looking around the building.

"Can you hold something for a minute?" Jeri asked, more estrogen in this building than she thought possible.

"Sure, yeah." Karla stepped over to the fence, her blonde hair all tied back into a knot at the nape of her neck, the perfect little side strands hanging down. She really belonged in a high-rise office building somewhere, and Jeri didn't usually like women like her.

But Karla put her hands on the fencing the way Scarlett did, and she did exactly what Jeri said. She got her hands dirty, and she smiled the whole time. So maybe she wasn't as bad as some of the women Jeri had previously known.

"All done," she said when she was only about halfway done. But the fencing would hold itself up until she got the rest nailed in place. "I'm assuming you two needed something."

"Yeah, you wouldn't come to the homestead for lunch, so I brought Karla to you."

Jeri paused, her eyes meeting Scarlett's. "I thought...I'm sorry. You didn't say what we'd be doing at lunch."

"Karla has an idea she wants to run by you." Scarlett smiled at Philo as he brought in his first load of equipment.

"We're considering building sort of a campsite on the ranch here. Cabins, really, where people can come stay, like in a hotel—but a cabin." Karla spoke a lot with her hands, gesturing around as if Jeri didn't understand the concept of cabin rentals.

"And they could have experiences with the animals, go down into town, whatever." Karla looked at Scarlett. "I want to put in a request for the money to several private organizations, as well as Forever Friends, but I have no idea what it takes to build something like that." Karla smiled at her. "I'm wondering if you can draw up some plans for a few different kinds of cabins, as well as a campsite map, and we can meet again."

Jeri felt the other woman's enthusiasm, and she actually shared it. "Sure," she said. "When do you need it by?"

"Whenever you've got it," Karla said. "But if we could get things out to people by the first of November, we'll catch them as they meet for their budget talks for next year."

"Oh, that's plenty of time." Jeri grinned at her. "I'll get it done quickly."

"Great." Karla smiled back at her, nodded at Scarlett, and left the building just as Philo brought in more equipment, along with his radio. He exited again, but Scarlett stayed.

"I suppose you want to talk about Sawyer," she said.

"Only if you want to."

Scarlett never had answered her text from that morning, so she didn't know what Scarlett had seen on the road that morning.

Jeri decided to go with complete denial. She shrugged, and said, "Not much to tell."

"That is *so* interesting," Scarlett said, a sparkle in her eyes. "Because Sawyer told Hudson that you two were *definitely* seeing each other."

Chapter Twelve

S awyer didn't hear from Jeri before lunch, so he didn't go to the homestead. When Hudson entered the barn where Sawyer worked, he kept tossing bales of straw onto the conveyor belt that went down to Dave, who loaded them onto the flatbed below. They had stalls in the pig barn to clean out, and then Sawyer would have to help Hudson with the horseshoeing.

So he'd have to see him them. But for now, Hudson just went about his work as usual. As the minutes passed, Sawyer relaxed, and when the flatbed had the required number of bales on it, he rode the conveyor down to Dave too.

His fingers ached a bit from all the gripping, but he clapped his hands together and got in the passenger seat of the truck. Dave got behind the wheel and started the truck. He checked his phone and said, "Oh, Scarlett wants me to stop by Gramps's place when we're done here." He stuck the phone back to the dashboard after tapping out a response.

"She say anything else?" Sawyer asked, unsure of why Scarlett would say anything to Dave about him.

"She wants me to help Gramps with some retirement account or something," he said. "I'm supposed to feed the llamas...." He glanced at Sawyer.

"I can do it," he said. "Then I'll help Hudson with the horseshoeing." He rolled the window down and enjoyed the breeze. "Why doesn't Scarlett have Sissy help Gramps?"

"Something about how she feels bad inflicting her personal problems on her professional accountant." Dave made a big show of rolling his eyes. "I don't have the degree, because I dropped out of college two semesters before finishing. So apparently I'm 'good enough.'"

"Ouch," Sawyer said with a chuckle.

"Yeah," Dave said, a bit darker than he usually was, cluing Sawyer into the fact that he was bothered by it.

"Just tell her you can't," Sawyer said. "We're swamped without Carson as it is."

"It's fine," Dave said, his own elbow resting on the windowsill as he drove down the road and around the corner. "I just hope Sissy isn't there like last time."

"I don't know her real well," Sawyer said. "You don't like her?"

"I like her fine," Dave said, but there was a falseness to his voice that hit Sawyer's radar. Maybe it was another

Carson-Adele situation, where they secretly liked each other but simultaneously annoyed the other just as much.

"Hey, I know this is super-bad timing," Dave said, glancing at Sawyer, and his heart sank all the way to the tips of his cowboy boots.

"What?"

"It's the first weekend of the month this weekend," he said, and Sawyer knew what came next.

"So you'll be at Fort Irwin." Sawyer sighed. "I'll arrange with Hudson to make sure the essentials are covered." It felt like he was back to trying to keep the ranch afloat by himself, though intellectually, he knew that wasn't even close to the truth. Since Scarlett and Adele had shown up with everything they owned in their cars, everything at Last Chance Ranch had improved.

"Cache will be here," he said. "And maybe Jeri could help out." Dave cut a look at Sawyer, and he couldn't decide if he knew something or was just seeing if Jeri could help out too.

"Maybe," Sawyer said, his voice a bit too high. He and Jeri had been married for almost two weeks now, and he'd never felt as self-conscious about the relationship until today. *Because you kissed her right out on the street,* he chastised himself.

"I know Scarlett's also increased the number of volunteer spots until our new help shows up."

"Hmm," Sawyer said. "But she needs a volunteer coordinator."

"Amber's doing it."

"And goat yoga? And all the goat care? And the dog-walking?"

"I guess," Dave said, obviously not nearly as concerned as Sawyer. Of course he wasn't. He was leaving this weekend, and Sawyer pushed away the jealousy. Surely Dave wouldn't be having a party during the one weekend of Army reserve training he attended each month.

He pulled up to the pig barn, and they both got out of the truck. "C'mon, Blue," he said to his dog who rode in the back. "Get out for a bit." The Australian shepherd jumped down, trotting over to the shade, where a water bowl sat.

Sawyer filled it up for his dog before starting to unload the bales of straw. He and Dave carried them into the barn and dropped them outside the stalls that needed done. The work took all of Sawyer's energy, especially when there were two of them trying to do the work of three men.

"Hey, my oven's on the fritz," Dave said. "Can I come cook something at your place tonight?"

Sawyer jerked his head up, panic parading through him. "Yeah, sure," he said, because before he and Jeri had started sharing their evenings together, having Dave borrow his oven wouldn't have been a problem. It wasn't a problem now.

"Jeri will probably be there," he said, bending to cut the twine on the straw.

"Jeri?" Dave paused with his pitchfork in his hand.

"Yeah, she's coming over tonight." Sawyer glanced at

Dave and went right on working. He wasn't going to be embarrassed about being interested in Jeri. She was beautiful, and he enjoyed his time with her immensely.

"Are you two...?"

"Yeah," Sawyer said, grinning at Dave. "Better find yourself someone," he added. "All the women up here will be gone."

Dave burst out laughing, the sound echoing throughout the barn. Sawyer let him carry on, even adding a chuckle himself.

"Yeah, no," Dave said.

"No?" Sawyer asked. "Why not?"

"I'm fine by myself."

Yeah, Sawyer had thought that too. But now, with Jeri... he realized what he'd been missing. "I'm just saying," he said. "Amber's cute. Or Sissy—"

"Did you seriously just suggest I go out with Sissy?" Dave asked. "We've, uh, done that." He ducked into another stall, his face turned away from Sawyer.

"You've been out with Sissy? When?" Sawyer wasn't sure why he cared. He normally didn't get involved in the gossip of the ranch, or in other relationships. He wouldn't want to talk about him and Jeri—hadn't he been stewing about that exact thing all day?

"Years ago," Dave said.

"So that's why you said you like her fine," Sawyer said.

"I do," Dave said. "I just don't want to go out with her."

He forked up another bunch of straw. "Or anyone. I don't need to be fixed up."

"Not a problem for me," Sawyer said.

"But good luck to you and Jeri," Dave said. "Seems like there's a lot of people around here making things work."

Considering how Carson had just left the ranch over a woman, Sawyer wasn't sure what Dave was talking about. It didn't matter. He still had miles to go before he'd be done with his chores, and if he had to share Jeri with Dave tonight, he definitely wanted to stop by the dog enclosure at some point.

Maybe sneak in a kiss. He was suddenly smiling, the lifting and pitching going much better now that he had a beautiful woman in the center of his mind.

He'd texted Jeri about Dave needing his oven, so she didn't come over at all. By the time Dave got his pizza out of the oven, ate it, and went home, Sawyer was cranky. He stepped out onto his back porch and sighed, gazing into the distance as the wind blew through the tops of the trees.

His back porch faced north, same as Carson's—well, the cabin that was empty now. He wondered if the new cowboy would take it or choose a different one. There were still five empty cabins in the Community, and Scarlett would do well to fill them all up.

He wished his porch faced the same direction as Jeri's,

but hers faced east. He could hear the clucking of her chickens, and then he heard the timbre of her voice as she talked to them.

Quickly, without thinking, he went down his step and around the corner of the house to find her sitting on the bottom step, throwing feed to her birds.

"Hey," he said, and she glanced up, the porch light illuminating her from behind.

"All done with dinner with your boyfriend?" she teased, and Sawyer scoffed as he crossed the lawn to join her on the steps.

"Can I sit with you?"

"If you want. I'm going to go in soon. I'm exhausted."

"Me too." He laced his fingers through hers, finally relaxing. "And we have to do it all again tomorrow."

She sighed and leaned her head against his shoulder. "Don't remind me."

"And Dave's going to his Army weekend in a few days," he said. "We might need to pull you over to the ranch side of things."

She groaned again, her hand tightening in his. "Fine, but make sure I'm with you."

He smiled into the darkness, glad she still wanted to spend time with him on the ranch. Darkness covered the twilight, and Sawyer enjoyed the silence with Jeri.

"Did you tell Hudson about us?" she asked, her voice quiet, barely above the clucking of her chickens.

"No," he said. "But Dave asked me about you, and I said we were seeing each other."

"Dave?"

"He wanted to come use my oven," Sawyer said. "I guess I wasn't thinking, because I said you'd probably be there, but he could come hang out."

"Then you texted me, and I didn't come."

"I didn't say you couldn't come."

"No, I know," she said. "He's not the one I'm worried about."

"Hudson said I told him?"

"No," Jeri said. "Scarlett came out the enclosure today. Said you told Hudson we were seeing each other."

A touch of frustration rose in his throat. "Are we hiding the relationship?"

"No," she said. "You kissed me in the middle of the road this morning."

"Yeah. That was nice." He sighed, laughing when she gave him a playful push. He lifted his arm and brought her close to him as they settled back to stillness. "So what are we doing?"

"I told Scarlett that we were seeing each other," Jeri said. "But that I didn't believe for a moment that you were gossiping about it to Hudson. I'm glad I was right."

"Yeah, I was just gossiping about it to Dave."

Jeri half scoffed and half laughed. "Yeah, I doubt it."

Sawyer pressed his lips to her temple. "Yeah, it wasn't gossip. I just said you might be there tonight, and he asked if we were dating, and I said yes. Then we talked about his Army weekend."

"Men and women are so different," she said with a little giggle. "If I'd have told my girlfriend I was dating you, I would've had to call for dinner and then breakfast while we discussed every little detail that had happened since the first time I saw you."

He laughed, the sound filling the sky. He couldn't remember the last time he'd laughed like this, and he sure did like it.

"Do you have girlfriends?" he asked.

"I used to," she said. "I could probably text Evelyn, and she'd drop everything to get together for lunch. She used to run my office."

"Wait a second," he said. "You told me you don't eat lunch."

She laughed this time, and Sawyer's pulse zinged around his body. "Well, I do with my girlfriends, obviously."

"What about your boyfriends?"

"Oh, cowboy, you're not my boyfriend." She twisted to look at him, and it was as if she'd captured the stars and put them in her eyes.

"Huh," he said, enjoying this game they were playing. Maybe too much. Or maybe he was just really out of practice and didn't know what was fun and flirty, and what wasn't. "I thought I was."

She kissed him, and Sawyer definitely felt like her boyfriend. Her touch was tender and passionate at the same time. "Mm," he said against her lips. "You taste like apples."

"Pink lady," she said, kissing him again.

"I thought you only ate freezer food," he teased, claiming her mouth again. She turned more fully toward him, and he felt a bit foolish making out with her on the back steps. He pulled back before he went too far and said, "Definitely your boyfriend."

"No," she said. "You're my husband."

Sawyer didn't feel like a husband, and he kept her close to him as he stared out into the night, wondering what would happen if he and Jeri really did make it far enough into their relationship to warrant marriage.

Could they get married all over again?

He didn't think so and at some point, their secret was going to become very, very public.

Chapter Thirteen

Joy came to Jeri as the weeks passed. She finished one dog enclosure and started on another, working with the dozens of moving parts it took to put a building up. From cement trucks to electricians to plumbers, Jeri managed them all by herself.

Honestly, she was exhausted, but she was doing what she loved, and that made up for it. When she wasn't eating dinner with Sawyer, or sitting on Sawyer's front porch holding his hand as they talked, or going to church with Sawyer, she worked on the sketches for Karla.

The cabins in the Community were functional for one person. She supposed a couple of people could live together if they got along really well. While there were two bedrooms, the living space was pretty small, and there was only one bathroom.

With the amount of hair Jeri had, if she'd had to share that tiny bathroom with someone else...it wouldn't go well.

So she put more into the cabins that could be built for a visitor. She knew the spice of life was variety, and she designed a studio cabin, with a fold down Murphy bed and a bigger bathroom. She also roughed out a one-bedroom cabin, with the same pull-down bed, bathroom, and full kitchen, but with a bit more room for the living area. And she had a third option, with two bedrooms and two bathrooms, a living room, kitchen, and pull-out bed for bigger families or groups.

All the cabins had a front porch and a back porch, as Jeri often thought homes overlooked their outdoor areas in favor of the indoor. But to her, outdoor living space was just as important as indoor. That area of the ranch had towering trees separating it from the homestead area, and it would be shady at certain parts of the day, so being outside would be a good option.

With those done, she turned her attention to the campsite itself. She knew it wasn't really for camping, but she wasn't sure if cabins counted as hotels. She'd taken to calling the area a glamping paradise, because glamorous camping had become a thing, to the point where in her research, she'd found a restoration company making glampers out of old model vans, buses, and campers.

There were magazines dedicated to glamping, Facebook groups, and pins of the cutest mini-houses someone could pull behind them, set up anywhere, and enjoy nature without breaking their back.

Jeri's back ached as she bent over her map, which was still quite bare. She'd been toying with putting in a spot for a campfire, but she worried about the animals on the ranch and all the smoke. Not to mention the people who lived here.

Honestly, Jeri wasn't so sure about putting in an area on the ranch where people could come stay. This ranch was an operational, living, breathing entity. They had over a hundred and fifty animals here now, with people in and out as it was to help take care of them.

They were a rescue ranch, and they already had people coming up to adopt the cats, dogs, pigs, llamas, and horses that were available.

She sighed and stretched, standing up to alleviate the pinch in her back. It was early in the morning, the sun not quite lighting the day. She'd tried working on the sketches at night, but she found it easier to start her day earlier than to burn the midnight oil.

Her phone chimed, odd for this time of day. She picked it up off the table where she'd been working and saw Scarlett's name on the screen.

You have mail, Scarlett had said. *I think it's your general contractors license. Can I open it?*

Jeri's heart suddenly beat in her ears. Her license had come—which meant she and Sawyer didn't need to stay married any longer.

It had been a couple of months.

Their time was up.

Sure, she tapped out.

Then I can scan it and get it to Jewel, her explanation came before Jeri could send her permission. She tapped send and let her hands fall back to her sides.

"This is it," she whispered to her cabin, the weight of the world landing on her shoulders.

She and Sawyer had been getting along so well. It was wonderful to have someone to talk to at night, and Jeri hadn't realized how much she missed something so simple.

She'd asked him to teach her how to play the guitar, and they'd joked about taking a cooking class together. He kissed her; she kissed him. He'd asked her to go to the Halloween carnival down the canyon in Pasadena, and she'd said yes though she hated dressing up.

He'd said he'd get her a cowgirl hat and a plaid shirt and they could be a country couple, and she'd laughed. She liked that he could make her laugh.

She swallowed, unsure of what to do. "You knew this day would come," she said to herself. "It was the deal."

So they could get a quiet divorce, just like they'd gotten secretly married. But she wasn't sure what that would do to their current relationship. She felt like someone had taken her life, put it in a blender, pushed the button, and walked away. They needed to come back and check on her. Make the upheaval stop.

Because now that she'd been on the ranch for a solid four months, and with Sawyer for two of those, she had no idea what she wanted. She hadn't hired someone to help her with the construction projects on the ranch. She hadn't thought she wanted to share her life with anyone, especially a man.

And yet...Sawyer wasn't just any man. She trusted him, and she grabbed her phone and started for the back door.

Are you up? she texted him.

Just got out of the shower.

She slowed her strides, her fantasies flying through her mind. *Text me when you're dressed. We need to talk.*

Oh boy, he texted back. *Are you breaking up with me?*

Jeri smiled at the same time she scoffed. She thought of him so often, she didn't even realize how far she'd fallen for him.

No, she said. *My license is here.*

Come on over.

She did, crossing her lawn and his and going up his back steps. She knocked at the same time she opened the door, and Blue was already there to greet her.

"Hey, bud," she said, scanning the living space in the cabin and finding it empty. "Where's your dad, huh?"

Blue didn't answer, of course, but they traded spots as she came in and he went out. She left the door ajar and went over to the kitchen counter, where Sawyer had already set a pot of coffee to brew. Already keyed up, she wasn't sure why she poured herself a cup, but she did.

He liked the stuff black, but she preferred cream and sugar, and he'd stocked his fridge for her.

For her.

Helplessness filled her, and she pressed her eyes closed. *What do I do?* she pleaded. *Help me know what to do.*

"Hey," Sawyer said. "You found the coffee, I see." He snaked his hand along her waist and kissed her forehead.

She leaned into his touch, tears heating the back of her eyes. *Tears.* Jeri couldn't remember the last time she'd cried, though the desperation and helplessness were familiar enough to remind her of why she'd decided to rebuild and then live her life alone.

Of course, she'd have business associates. Friends she kept at a distance. People she worked with and for.

But Sawyer had broken all of those barriers, and she hadn't even realized it until Scarlett's text had come in.

One thing she knew: This wasn't a game to her. Nor to him.

She faced him, needing to know how he truly felt about things. "What are we going to do?"

He gazed evenly back at her. "I don't know." At least he was honest.

"What do you *want* to do?"

He ducked his head, but he wasn't wearing his cowboy hat, and she'd seen him do this before anyway. He fiddled with the spoon on the countertop, making a metallic clinking noise in the silence between them.

"Hey." She ran her hand up his arm to his face. He pressed into her touch too, and Jeri wasn't sure she'd ever known a man as sweet as Sawyer. "Tell me."

He looked at her again. "I want—" His voice sounded rough, rusty, ragged. He sighed, breathed in, and tried again.

"I just want you," he said, his dark hazel eyes like pools of the prettiest pond water. They were wide open, and vulnerable, and Jeri inched closer to him and kissed him.

It didn't feel like a last kiss or a good-bye kiss. If anything, this slow, unrushed kiss held more love and passion than any of their others, and there had been some truly spectacular kisses between them.

"I don't want to lose you," he whispered. He was saying and doing all the right things, and while Jeri's confusion and frustration with the situation remained, one thing trumped them all.

Her love for Sawyer.

She pulled back but stayed right in his personal space. "Can we just stay married?" Was that even possible? Why didn't it feel as crazy as it sounded?

Sawyer kissed her again, said, "Sure," and led her into the more private areas of his cabin.

JERI ACTUALLY TOOK a lunch hour that day, deciding she didn't have to work ten hours a day without food. She *chose* to do that, just like she and Sawyer had chosen to stay married even though it wasn't necessary anymore. A lot of choices had been made that morning, in fact, and Jeri didn't regret any of them.

She rang the doorbell at the homestead, having just texted Scarlett to see if she'd be there. She'd messaged back to say she was out in Karla's cabin, but could run over. So when Jeri heard, "Come in!" in Scarlett's voice, she went right in.

"Hey," Jeri said, smiling at her boss. "I just came to get the license."

Scarlett twisted from where she stood at the sink. "Come on in. I just raided Gramps's freezer and got some of Adele's leftovers." She smiled, but Jeri knew Scarlett missed her best friend.

"How is Adele?" Jeri asked, wondering what was rotating in the microwave. Her stomach growled, but she usually just satisfied it with water or a sports drink, and she didn't need anything heavy.

"She seems to be doing okay." Scarlett finished washing her hands and turned to wipe them on a towel. "I hope she comes back, though. I've tried tempting her with a ranch chef job, but so far, no luck." She popped open the microwave and pulled out a steaming bowl. "Luckily, we have her chicken corn chowder to remember her by."

Jeri laughed. "Chicken corn chowder, wow."

"Right?" Scarlett got down a couple of bowls and opened a drawer for silverware.

"I don't eat a lot at lunch," Jeri said as the other woman started to ladle soup into a bowl. "So just a little for me."

"I know," Scarlett said. "You don't take a lunch hour."

She looked at Jeri, her eyes sharp and sinking in. "So why'd you take one today?"

Jeri shrugged. "I've decided that maybe I don't need to work so much."

"I've been telling you that for months."

"I know," Jeri said, accepting the spoon and bowl of soup. "But I'm stubborn, and sometimes I just need to come to things on my own."

"Mm hm." Scarlett came around the island and sat at the bar beside Jeri, something glinting on her left hand.

"Oh my stars in heaven," Jeri said, grabbing her friend's hand and staring at the diamond ring. "Hudson proposed."

Scarlett giggled and held her hand out to admire it. "He did."

"You said yes."

"I did." She gave Jeri a look out of the side of her eye, and it was casual and yet Jeri felt like Scarlett had so much more to say.

She took a bite of her soup, wishing she and Sawyer had talked a bit more about what to tell their friends around the ranch. Of course, nothing they'd done that morning should really be talked about with anyone.

And Scarlett said nothing. She simply ate, and though she had more soup than Jeri, she finished first. Jeri could barely put food in her mouth, as the truth seemed to be filling it, making swallowing difficult.

She got up from the counter when Scarlett did, even though her bowl wasn't empty. Scarlett let her wash out her bowl and put it in the dishwasher without comment, and the silence was driving Jeri toward madness.

"Okay," she finally said. "What do you want to know?"

"What?" Scarlett asked, but it was a little too innocent.

Jeri grinned and shook her head. "Come on. I can tell you're dying to ask me something. Or say something. Whatever. Just say it."

Instead of speaking, Scarlett stepped over to the built-in desk that held papers and folders and plucked one from the pile. "This is your license," she said, extending it to Jeri.

Jeri reached for it, but Scarlett snapped it back at the last moment. She peered at it as if she hadn't already seen it. "I found it quite interesting that the last name is Smith." She looked at Jeri again, her eyes downright eagle-like. "Same as one Sawyer Smith, cowboy here at the ranch."

Jeri swallowed, a totally amateur move for someone trying to keep a secret. "It's a common last name," she said.

"And yet." Scarlett hit the T-sound hard. "Your W-9 and employment paperwork has the last name of Bell on it." She folded the contractor's license and carefully placed it back in the envelope it had come in. "So which is it, Jeri?" Her eyes blazed with a mixture of curiosity, amusement, and perhaps some annoyance. Jeri supposed she'd be irritated if someone she'd hired and trusted had lied to her.

But Jeri hadn't lied. "I was—both sets of paperwork are correct," she said.

"You have two last names?" Scarlett folded her arms,

tucking the envelope under one of them, making it seem very far out of Jeri's reach.

Jeri scrambled for something else to say, but nothing came to mind. Time to tell the truth.

She sighed, letting Scarlett know she didn't appreciate this conversation. But she and Sawyer had kept the secret for two months now, and if she wanted any kind of future with him—which she honestly couldn't believe she did—she couldn't put him in a situation that would compromise his morals.

She didn't want to compromise hers either.

"It's a long story," she said.

"Give me the cliff notes," Scarlett said. "I'm interviewing a few more cowboys in twenty minutes."

Twenty minutes. Jeri could survive the next twenty minutes. "All right. Cliff notes. At the beginning of this year, there was an accident at one of my construction sites. It wasn't my fault, but my foreman blamed it on me. I lost my crew. My company. Everything—including my license."

Scarlett's eyes rounded, the playfulness disappearing from them. "Jeri. You're kidding."

"I wish," she said. "I took a few months off, trying to get my license back. There was an official hearing and everything. I was denied. When this job came up, and I bid on it, I only did it because it was Last Chance Ranch, and I did have a provisional license at the time. It felt like maybe if I could get the job here, it would be my last chance." Her emotions swelled, and she looked away from Scarlett, worried she might actually cry.

She cleared her throat as Scarlett stepped over and wrapped her in a warm hug. "I'm sorry."

"It gets worse."

Scarlett stepped back. "You didn't have a license until now," she said, setting the envelope on the counter.

"No, I lost the temporary after I was hired here," Jeri said, not sure she could continue. Scarlett knew anyway, so she gestured with her hand to go on.

"You married Sawyer to get a new last name and applied for a new license with that."

Jeri nodded.

"Holy crap, Jeri." Scarlett's face burst into a smile. "I can't believe this." She looked like she'd been lit up like a Christmas tree. "So...I mean, are you two...?"

"We're dating," Jeri said, deciding her boss didn't need to know everything. "It was just going to be for a couple of months. He only agreed to it for the ranch, so we could get the funding from Forever Friends. We didn't—I didn't want you to lose that. I couldn't do that to you, and I wanted the job, and—" She cut off, starting to feel desperate, and she didn't want this to be about her.

Though, of course, it was all about her.

She stared at Scarlett, hoping her boss would understand. She felt like she was teetering on the edge of a cliff, her job, her cabin, her future at the ranch only a toe away from going over.

"I understand why you did it," she finally said. "And Jewel won't need to know. She just needed the license for her file, and now she has it."

Jeri nodded, her mouth feeling slimy and thick. "Thank you, Scarlett."

"And you and Sawyer...now what?" Scarlett asked.

Jeri thought about the slow, perfect way he'd loved her that morning. "We're still working on that part."

Scarlett looked worried, and Jeri wasn't sure why. "Why are you concerned?"

"Because I need you both," Scarlett said. "I can't lose Sawyer the way I lost Carson, and I can't lose you either. I'm just...if you guys break-up, will one of you leave the ranch?"

Jeri didn't know the answer to that question either. There were too many new things going on in her life for her to process them all, including her new and deep feelings for Sawyer when she'd thought she'd never want another man in her life.

"I don't know," she said. "But I promise I won't leave you high and dry."

Scarlett nodded, and Jeri picked up her license and said, "I have to get back to work," hoping she could keep that promise.

Chapter Fourteen

It didn't take much for Sawyer to get used to his new morning routine—one where he woke with the slumbering form of Jeri beside him. In his cabin, in his bed.

He gazed at her, the love he felt for her swirling through him lazily, the way the breeze lilted around the ranch in the summer.

Of course, it was fall now, and heading into winter, and the breeze had morphed into wind. He didn't mind it, as it was still plenty warm, and the wind blew some of the more offensive ranch smells to the east.

He reached over and tucked Jeri's hair behind her ear, causing her to shift and groan. "Why are you waking me up so early on a weekend?" she asked, her eyes still closed.

He chuckled and brought his hand back to his side of the bed. "Habit," he said.

"It's Saturday," she said, rolling over so her back was to him.

Unfortunately, his body didn't have different internal alarms for weekdays and weekends. He got out of bed and said, "I have a couple of chores this morning before we go to the carnival."

"Mm," Jeri said, and Sawyer knew she'd fall back asleep to the sound of the shower. She'd told him she loved that sound, as it soothed her back to sleep. She was the opposite of him in that arena.

Once he was awake, he couldn't go back to sleep. But she could, almost at the drop of a hat. He placed a kiss on her forehead and went into the bathroom. He turned the shower on first so she'd have a few extra minutes of the noise and then got out his toothbrush.

Looking at himself in the mirror, he hardly recognized himself. His hair was much longer than he normally kept it, but he hadn't cut it because Jeri said she loved the way it curled around his ears. He liked how she ran her fingers through it as he kissed her, but he did look different without his military cut.

He'd grown a beard over the past couple of weeks too, but that was mostly because he and Jeri were sharing a bathroom now and trying to get out the door at the same time, and he'd missed a few days of shaving. It fit his theme for Halloween, so he'd gone with it. He'd even told her he'd grown it on purpose, so her feelings wouldn't get hurt about how long it took her to get ready in the morning.

Sawyer was doing all kinds of things he'd never done before. Things he hadn't even known he wanted to do—like share his personal space with someone. Tell them about his day. Express his thoughts, his hardships, his dreams.

Jeri had told Scarlett about them, about the marriage. Hudson knew too, but neither of them had said anything to Sawyer. Cache, Dave, Lance, and another new cowboy Scarlett had just brought on—Ames Golden—didn't seem to care what Sawyer and Jeri did. He got his work done on the ranch, as did they, and everything was fine.

He rinsed his mouth and looked back into his eyes. He'd been trying to pinpoint what about himself looked different besides the hair and beard. There was something in his eyes.

"Happiness," he whispered to his reflection. He was happier now than he'd ever been in his life, and that could change a man.

After showering, he dressed while Jeri slept, and he stepped over to her and kissed her quickly. "We're leaving for the carnival at eleven," he whispered, tracking his lips down the side of her neck as a final good-bye. She smelled sweet, like fresh cotton and those pink lady apples she loved.

She sighed, and he chuckled. "See you later, sweetheart."

Jeri grabbed onto his collar and pulled him in for another kiss, this one much longer and deeper.

"I have to go," he said against her mouth, not wanting to go anywhere.

"Go then," she said, but she claimed his lips again, and he didn't pull away.

You're going to be so late, he thought, but then he decided he didn't care.

BY THE TIME Sawyer and Jeri arrived at the carnival, he knew they'd have to wait in line forever to get lunch from one of the stands.

"This is insane," she said, gazing around. "I had no idea."

Sawyer did. He'd been to this carnival before, and it seemed every citizen of Pasadena showed up to it. "We can go somewhere else for food."

Jeri hooked her arm through his. "I don't think we need to do that."

Sawyer suppressed his sigh. "All right. What do you want to eat?"

"Sissy and Karla said the chili is the best," Jeri said.

"Are they here already?"

"Yeah," Jeri said, adjusting her sunglasses and her cowgirl hat. "They got here earlier."

Like we should've, Sawyer thought, quickly pushing the thought away. It was as much his fault as hers that he hadn't gotten out the door on time that morning.

"We're meeting them for the show," Jeri said, getting in the astronomically long line for chili and cornbread. Sawyer watched as a family of six walked by, the kids with orange and black balloons tied around their wrists, and the baby in the stroller crying. The mother and father didn't seem to notice the wailing at all. A sense of longing he didn't understand cascaded through him.

"Right, the show," he said, turning back to Jeri. "I can't believe Cache, Lance, and Dave are doing that."

"Have you heard them?" she asked. "They're really good."

Apparently, the other men on the ranch had started a band while Sawyer had been occupied with Jeri and his ranch work. He wasn't jealous exactly, but he felt a bit left out. He didn't want to hang out with men when Jeri was available, but he didn't want to completely feel like he didn't belong with his friends either.

Everything was so new to him, and he didn't know how to make sense of all of it. So he waited in line and listened to Jeri talk about the upcoming Thanksgiving dinner at the ranch.

"So do you want to go see your parents?" she asked. "Or stay at the ranch?"

"I'll talk to my mom," he said, distracted by another family passing them. "Jeri?" he asked, watching the dark-eyed little girl lick an ice cream cone. "Do you want more kids?"

She flinched toward him, her own dark eyes filled with shock. She searched his face, and he had his answer. It was still hard for him to hear her say, "No."

"Why not?" He inched forward with the line. "It might be different this time."

"Why would it be different?"

"Because, once again, I'm not Howie." He looked evenly back at her. "And you're not twenty-one-years-old anymore."

"Exactly," she said. "I'm too old to have babies, Sawyer."

He looked away. "There's adoption."

"Hey." She guided his face back to hers, but he felt like a fool and could barely look at her. This conversation was too heavy for a Halloween carnival, for the chili line with so many people around. "Do *you* want kids?"

"Well, yeah," he said. "I mean, I wouldn't mind having kids."

"I guess I just assumed you knew...I didn't."

"Why would I assume that?"

"Because I have a son who ignores me when I call on his birthday?" Jeri's eyes blazed now, and she was definitely angry.

"Yeah," Sawyer said, his insides twisting and twisting. "It's fine."

Jeri didn't say anything else, and the silence between them wasn't as comfortable as it usually was. They got their chili, and Jeri pulled out her phone and dialed someone. "Hey, we're here. Where are you guys?"

A few minutes later, they found their friends from the ranch, and Jeri slid onto the bench of the picnic table beside

Amber, who seemed to have as much hair as Jeri, only in a much lighter shade.

Of the three women they'd joined, only Sissy had dressed up. She wore all black, with a pair of cat ears on her head and a tail hanging off the waist of her shorts. Karla was much too sophisticated to dress up, and she wore the same thing Sawyer had always seen her in. A pair of khaki shorts and a blouse, with huge earrings and a smile on her face.

She felt a bit plastic to him, but he didn't interact with her much and had tried not to judge. Amber could probably pass for a princess, what with the long, purple dress she wore and the flower crown she had in her hair.

In fact, she probably had intentionally dressed up as a princess. He said hello to all of them, and they flashed smiles and greetings back at him.

Jeri immediately engrossed herself in a conversation with the other women while Sawyer sat there and ate his barely warm chili. He wasn't feeling much like carnival-ing, but he put on a good front and smiled when it was time to take selfies with his girlfriend.

Wife, he reminded himself. She hadn't exactly moved all of her stuff to his place, but she came over at night and stayed until morning. She had toiletries there, and in the three weeks since she'd gotten her contractor's license, when she brought groceries, they went in his fridge.

He wandered through the craft booths with the women while they passed time until the show. He cheered and clapped for his cowboy friends as they took the stage.

Dave stepped right up to the mic like he was born with one in his hand, and he said, "We're the Last Chance Cowboys," with a wide smile. "Let's go, boys."

He and Cache started playing their guitars at the same time, and the jealousy punched Sawyer in the gut this time. He could play guitar too. Jeri had even asked him to teach her how. And yet, no one on the stage had said anything to him about a band. He'd been at Last Chance Ranch longer than all of them—longer than anyone—and if there was someone who was a Last Chance Cowboy, it was him.

The Last Chance Cowboys definitely sounded country, and Sawyer could admit that Dave could sing really well.

So can you, a voice whispered in Sawyer's head, and he tried to quiet it. It disappeared for a moment, but then it returned, seething and whispering right beneath his skin.

Lance played drums and sang harmony vocals, and at some point, there was three-part harmony. Beside him, Jeri clapped along, whooping when the song ended. She tuned to him with pure energy on her face. "They're so great, right?"

"Yeah," he yelled over the applause. "So great."

And they were—and once again, Sawyer didn't recognize this new version of himself. Didn't know who he was. And he certainly didn't like how he felt.

The bigger problem was he had no idea what to do about any of it.

Is this just my life now? he wondered. He turned his thoughts toward the Lord. *Is this what I'm doing now?*

Feeling jealous and left out from something I probably wouldn't want to do anyway?

But he hadn't even been asked. He hadn't even known about the band until a few days ago. He wasn't the only cowboy on the ranch that wasn't in it, but it still felt like he was. It was as if an invisible wall had been put up between him and everyone else, and he wasn't sure if he'd built it or how to get it down.

When he was alone with Jeri, the wall wasn't there, and he liked that. Maybe that was why he liked her so much. Why he *loved* her.

The band started up again, and Sawyer went through the motions of clapping the way everyone else did.

But his thoughts refused to be distracted by good country music, and he couldn't help thinking that maybe, just maybe, he'd fallen too fast for Jeri Bell. That maybe, just maybe, he shouldn't have married her. That maybe, just maybe, he'd done it to feel like a hero when he was anything but.

Chapter Fifteen

Jeri felt the shift in her and Sawyer's relationship, but she couldn't pinpoint when it had happened. Maybe at the carnival when she'd told him she didn't want kids. But no, she shook her head as she fitted the ceiling tiles into place. It was before that.

A couple of weeks had passed since that chili-line conversation, and yet she thought about it every day. At church on Sunday, children had consumed her thoughts, and she'd asked God if she should want to be a mother.

Growing up, it had been something she'd wanted. She'd been determined to show her family that each member was important, not just the ones that came along at the right time. And yet, she'd walked away from Randy when her ex-husband had asked her to.

She was worse than her parents.

So no, she didn't want more kids.

She wasn't sure if that was the strain on them or not. She knew if they weren't married already, they wouldn't be living the way they were, and she sighed into the steps she took down the ladder.

"So what?" she asked the air conditioned building. "I move back to my place and pretend we...pretend what, exactly?"

The empty enclosure didn't have an answer, but it seemed the Lord did. Jeri felt that yes, she should not sleep over at Sawyer's anymore. Go see him at night, sure. Kiss him good-night when she left, sure. But just because they had a piece of paper with the right information on it didn't mean they were ready for everything a marriage entailed.

She climbed the ladder again and put the ceiling tile in place, feeling calmer than she had since the carnival. She didn't want to wait to talk to Sawyer, and she didn't think this conversation should happen through a device.

Deciding the ceiling could wait, she got down and went outside. This was the third enclosure out of five, and she was proud of how they'd come together. They were similar in shape to the existing enclosures, but these new ones were larger, with better materials.

The sound of barking dogs entered her awareness, something she usually just ignored as she worked in the Canine Club and dealt with barking all day long. But today, she walked over to the yard where most of the dogs spent the day outside. They still locked all the animals down at night due to the coyotes, but everyone got to roam outside during the day.

Maybe she needed a dog. Amber ran the volunteers and the adoption programs, and Jeri had become friends with her over the weeks. They both had a huge mop of hair, and that had resulted in some Saturday afternoons of talk about how to deal with it, usually with one of their favorite snacks.

Jeri took chips and salsa, and Amber always had fruity candy. Jeri's mouth watered from the sour Skittles she'd had a few days ago, reminding herself that she couldn't really take care of a dog.

But there was no reason she couldn't take one home with her at night and put it back in the huge dog pen while she worked. Inside enclosure three, which was actually the closest one to the road, she found one of the ranch's employees writing on a clipboard.

"Oh, hello, Jeri," Genevieve said, looking up. "Here to look at the building?"

"I'm actually thinking about adopting a dog," she said. "Can I just walk around?"

Genevieve wore surprise on her face, but she blinked it away quickly. "Yeah, I can take you out into the yard." She hung the clipboard on the nail by the door and jangled a huge ring of keys. "Something big or small? Well, medium. Our small dogs go so fast, and I don't think we have one anymore."

"Why is small better than big?" Jeri asked.

"Easier to take care of," she said. "Easier to walk. Easier

to pick up. Easier to have sleep in bed with you at night." She flashed a smile in Jeri's direction. "What are you looking for?"

"I'm not sure," Jeri said, because she hadn't considered size one of the things that would eliminate a dog from a possible adoption.

"Well, Sawyer has that Australian shepherd. He's a pretty decent size. Probably forty pounds?" Genevieve looked at Jeri with her eyebrows raised, but Jeri's mind had blanked. Genevieve kept talking, but her voice echoed now.

"I'm sorry," she finally said, realizing they'd stepped outside. Jeri didn't even know she'd done that. "Why does Sawyer's dog have anything to do with what I get?"

"Well, you live with him, right?" Genevieve looked at her, her blue eyes innocent yet curious at the same time.

"No," Jeri said. "I have my own cabin."

"Oh." Genevieve blinked rapidly. "I—"

"Why did you think we lived together?"

"Uh...." Genevieve looked away like one of the pups that had come over to her might save her from this conversation. "I went out with Dave a couple of times. He told me you guys were married."

The breath left Jeri's body, and she wasn't even sure why. She and Sawyer *were* married. She was practically living with him, though she still had dishes and clothes and tools—and her chickens—at her cabin.

Did married people think about themselves as living with someone?

Jeri's feelings about needing to put some distance between her and Sawyer until they were really ready to be married roared back to life, and she turned back to the door. "I'm sorry. I forgot I need to call my electrician. I don't have time to look at dogs right now." She had to wait for Genevieve to unlock the door and let her back in, and then Jeri practically ran from enclosure three.

She didn't go straight over to the area of the ranch where she'd most likely find Sawyer. He worked in LlamaLand, or Piggy Paradise, or Horse Heaven. But she went back to her cabin, too afraid to face him in that moment and tell him that she didn't think she'd ever be ready to be married to him for real.

She called her electrician, because she didn't want to be a liar—there was already too many other things she'd been keeping secret, including things she hadn't even admitted to herself.

JERI FOUND Sawyer coming back to the heart of the ranch along the road bordering the llama pastures. She'd loitered around the barns and stables for about twenty minutes before just calling him.

He'd said he'd be in soon, and she'd stayed in the shade until she saw him walking along the fence, tapping the posts every now and then. Her feelings rose up and choked her, but she remained firm in her resolve.

She pushed away from the stable where she'd been keeping cool and started toward him. Maybe the conversation would be easier under the open sky, away from anyone who might need to go in and out of the stable.

Sawyer heard her footsteps as she neared, and he glanced up. His smile still came quickly, but she could just feel the tension between them. "Hey, beautiful," he said.

Warmth spread through her, and she smiled back at him. "Hey."

"What's going on? You sounded a little upset on the phone."

"I'm not upset," she said. "I'm...." She had no idea what she was. How she felt. It was impossible to separate all the threads of her emotions. "I need to move back into my own cabin."

He blinked and reached up to adjust his cowboy hat lower on his head. "I wasn't aware you'd moved out of your cabin."

"Oh, come on, Sawyer," she said. "I haven't slept there in weeks." She glanced left and right like she couldn't even be seen talking to him. "One of the enclosure workers knows we're married, and I feel...."

"What?" he asked, meeting her eyes now. "How do you feel?"

"I feel stupid," she said, admitting it. "I didn't mean—I mean—I don't think." She sighed. "Look, if we weren't married, I wouldn't be sleeping over. We'd just be dating still, and learning about each other, and it would be a long time before we got married. I just don't think—"

"You think it would be a long time before we got married?" True surprise ran through his expression.

Of course it did. Jeri hadn't shared any of her ill will toward marriage with him. He knew her first marriage had not gone well or ended well, and he knew her last boyfriend had betrayed her and cost her everything.

But he didn't know that she'd vowed never to tie herself to someone who could hurt her again. Not emotionally and spiritually the way Howie had. Not mentally and physically the way Brenden had.

"Look," she said, breathing in deeply. "I just think maybe we rushed into, you know, living the married life."

"So you don't want to be married anymore." Sawyer squinted at her, clearly trying to figure out what she wanted.

Join the club, she wanted to tell him.

"No," she said. "I think everything would be better if we weren't married anymore."

Something flashed across his face, and it looked very much like anger. "That's easy, Jeri," he said. "I'll take care of it." He started to walk away, but Jeri reached out and grabbed his arm.

"Wait," she said. "I can take care of it."

"Aren't you three days behind on the most recent enclosure?"

The fact that he knew that touched her heart. He listened to her when she talked to him at night, even if he didn't add a lot to the conversation. "Yes, but I can do it. You only married me to help me, and you shouldn't have to pay for it, or take your time to do it."

He nodded. "Fine." He gently drew his arm away from her hand. "I hope we can still be friends." He took a couple of steps before Jeri's brain caught up to what he'd said.

She jumped in front of him. "What does that mean? Of course we're going to be friends. I still want you to be my *boy*friend."

Didn't she?

Yes. Yes, she did.

She cared about Sawyer a lot. On some level, she loved him. She'd loved Howie too, when they'd gotten married. But was it the kind of love Scarlett and Hudson enjoyed? Jeri didn't think they were even close to being on the same level as that.

Yet, her mind whispered, but she tried to kick the thought out. It scared her too much, and she needed more time to accept the fact that she'd already opened herself up for more pain.

"Jeri." Sawyer shook his head. "I think you already know this, but I'm going to say it anyway. I love you."

She shook her head, tears gathering in the back of her throat. "Don't. Things haven't been right between us for weeks."

"And yet, I'm still here," he said. "So are you. That says something, don't you think?"

She sighed and looked away. "I don't know, Sawyer."

He pressed a kiss to her cheek, his lips lingering a little too long. "I don't know a whole lot, either, Jeri. But if you want to move back to your place, that's fine with me. If you want to get divorced, I guess I'm okay with that." He kept his face close to hers so she couldn't see his eyes.

In fact, he ducked his head closer to her neck. "I don't like it, because I think we're great together. But I think you might be right in saying we may have rushed into living a married life. And because I respect you and hope you'll want to marry me again for real again, I'll do whatever you want."

Her breath stuck in her throat.

"See you later for dinner?" he asked.

She nodded, because she couldn't speak, and Sawyer sauntered away as if they hadn't just had the hardest conversation of their relationship.

Jeri spun away from him, suddenly second-guessing everything she'd ever felt and thought.

What if she'd just made the biggest mistake of her life?

Chapter Sixteen

Sawyer hated eating by himself after having Jeri with him for the past couple of months. But she'd left the ranch—he knew, because the car that usually sat in her driveway was gone.

It had been gone when he'd finished his chores and returned to his cabin, as had all of her personal belongings in his cabin. He'd stopped in the doorway of the bedroom, noticing how stark and square everything was without her jewelry on the dresser or her clothes hanging in his closet.

His closet.

Just his.

He'd just taken a bite of Swedish meatballs when his phone rang. His heart thumped out a beat of adrenaline when he saw Jeri's name. He swallowed his food while it was still too big, making his throat rebel in protest.

But he was able to say, "Hello," before the call went to voicemail.

"Okay, so we have a problem," she said in a hushed tone. Not even a hello. Sawyer didn't care. He just wanted her to come back to him.

Even if she only wants to be your girlfriend forever?

Yeah, he didn't like that. Not even a little bit. But the way she spoke about marriage, he'd gotten the impression that she didn't even want a real husband. But a make-believe one was okay, even if she did real married things with him.

He shook the poisonous thoughts out of his head. "Problem?"

"It takes six months to get divorced in California," she said. "There's a mandatory waiting period."

"Oh."

"So I looked into an annulment, and we could do that."

"What's the difference?" he asked.

"There are some stipulations to an annulment," she said. "But it basically recognizes the marriage as never having existed."

"Which is easier?"

"Well...the annulment would be easier—at first. You'd have to come to court, though, and explain the fraud you've learned about. You know, so I could just get my license with your name."

Sawyer closed his eyes. "I don't want to go to court." And he didn't want to tell anyone about their plan. In his mind, their marriage wasn't fraudulent. Or fake—and that was the real problem. "I suppose we should've done some research about ending the marriage."

"I suppose," she said. "So just a divorce?"

"Yes, please," he said, his heart wailing against the prospect.

"Okay," she said.

Before she could hang up, he asked, "Where are you?"

"Pasadena."

"I'm surprised the offices aren't closed."

"Just a few more minutes," she said. "Can I call you later?"

"Sure." He hung up, the resulting silence surrounding him too deep and too wide for him to survive. He got up and went outside, the strains of guitar and drums coming from Cache's cabin next door.

Sawyer didn't think; he went down the steps, Blue at his side, and crossed over to Cache's house. Knocking loudly on the door, he called, "Can I come in?"

The music stopped, and a few moments later, Cache opened the door. He still wore his work clothes and boots, but he had a guitar strapped over his shoulder. "Sawyer," he said, surprised.

He wore the same military hair cut Sawyer usually did, and he had the sudden urge to get his hair cut instead of hanging out with a band he wasn't part of. "Hey," he said, swallowing. "Wondering if I can come hang out with you tonight."

"Sure." Cache grinned at him. "It's just me and Lance. Dave has a date."

"Another one," Lance called from further inside the cabin.

"He goes out a lot," Cache said.

"Yeah, I've noticed," Sawyer said, stepping in. "I can stand in for him if you have music."

"That would be great," Cache said, closing the door behind him. "Where's Jeri tonight?"

"In town," he said evasively. He faced the two cowboys. "Can I ask you guys a question?"

"Sure," Cache said again, exchanging a glance with Lance. Sawyer liked Lance, who had sandy blonde hair and the longest sideburns he'd ever seen. But he could get any animal to do what he wanted, and he worked hard.

"Did you guys know Jeri and I got married?"

Another exchanged glance. "Yes," they said together.

"How'd you find out?"

"I don't remember," Cache said. "Everyone just knows."

Everyone just knows. Sawyer ground his teeth together and spied a guitar leaning against the wall. "Let's just play. May I?" He indicated the instrument, and Cache nodded, an edge of fear in his eyes now.

"Music's right there."

"Thanks." Sawyer stepped over to the music stand and focused on the notes. "I think I can do this." He let his fingers drip over the strings, and this guitar was much nicer than his.

"All right," Cache said. "Let's play, boys."

Sawyer looked at him, and he nodded. Sawyer played with him, feeling some of the tension and frustration leak away with the song.

SUNDAY MORNING, Sawyer drove to church himself. He'd been going with Jeri, but he'd signed the divorce papers on Thursday, and they hadn't spoken that much since. She'd said she still wanted him to be her boyfriend, but she'd gone to town for groceries of her own on Thursday night, and back down with all the women at the ranch on Friday night.

She'd been sick on Saturday, and he'd taken her some soup from Karla, who'd been cooking for the ranch since she'd arrived. Scarlett had cried through one of the lunches a few weeks ago, and Sawyer had steered clear of that. Jeri had told him that all the cooking and food reminded her of Adele, and it was hard for Scarlett to be here without her best friend.

Sawyer felt like he understood Scarlett on a new level now, as he parked in the church lot and looked at the steeple. He wasn't sure how he could keep living at Last Chance Ranch with Jeri next door. So close, and yet so blasted far away.

The minutes passed, and he didn't go inside. Other people started to arrive, and still he remained in the truck.

"Have I done something wrong?" he asked, his question directed toward God.

He didn't think he had, but he'd lost Jeri, something he'd told her he specifically didn't want.

"Maybe she just doesn't love me the same way I love her." Maybe he'd fallen too fast. Maybe he was in a better emotional state than she was. No matter what, he knew a couple of things.

He hadn't done anything wrong, as the peace filling him testified to him.

And Jeri definitely needed more time to get to the same place he was already in.

So could he be patient?

He decided he could, and he got out of the truck and went in to listen to Pastor Williams' sermon.

THINGS between him and Jeri improved over the next couple of weeks. She returned to his cabin in the evenings. They ate dinner together and talked about their day, their pets, their work, their dreams.

Well, he talked about his dreams. Jeri never had said all that much about what she wanted, even when he'd asked her. And asked her. He wanted to press the issue, but he felt like he already had, so he'd let it drop. For now.

They'd decided to stay at Last Chance Ranch for Thanksgiving, and the night before the big dinner, she brought extra stuffing to his cabin to go with the chicken he'd grilled.

"This just has to go in the oven for forty minutes," she said.

"Well, if there's one thing we can do, it's stick something in the oven." He smiled at her, glad she was here. "Chicken's almost done, but I can put foil over it."

She put the stuffing in the oven while he went down the back steps. She joined him a few moments later, her presence a blessing in his life, whether she was his wife or not.

"I have to tell you something," she said.

He glanced down at her, suspicious of the serious tone. "All right."

"I'd like to go to Eugene for the holidays." She turned toward him, determination blazing in her eyes. At least he thought it was determination.

When her tears fell, he realized how wrong he was.

"Oh, don't cry," he said, mostly because he had no idea how to deal with a crying woman. He wrapped her in his arms, and she melted into him. "What's wrong?"

"You know how you've asked me what my dreams are? What I want for my life?"

"Yes," he said, rubbing slow circles along her back and wondering where she was going to go with this. Why her dreams upset her and led her to Eugene, Oregon.

"I've been thinking a lot about it." She stepped out of his arms and wiped her face before focusing on the ground. "And there are some things I want."

"Okay," he said when she didn't continue. "What are they?"

"I'd rather not say quite yet."

"But you're going to Eugene to get them," he said, his mind working quickly. "Your family?"

"Just my son," she said, her fingers braiding and unbraiding themselves. "I have a lot of regrets from that part of my life, and I don't think...I can ignore them any longer."

Sawyer nodded, understanding filling him. "You do what you need to do. I'll go to Newport Beach and tell my parents we broke up."

A moment of horror crossed her face. "Really?"

"No?"

"Why do they have to think we broke up? We're still together." She tipped forward slightly, looking up under the brim of his hat. "Right? We're still together?"

"Yes," he said. "Of course we're still together." He'd been the one who'd needed the reassurance these past few weeks, and Jeri had given him that. While he really liked her in his cabin with him, there was something exciting about seeing her in the evening, kissing her, and sending her home too.

He didn't want to date forever, but for now, it was okay.

"I want to...." She trailed off and looked at the smoke rising from the grill. He turned to it and lifted the lid to give himself something else to focus on. Jeri usually didn't have a problem saying what she wanted to say, but sometimes

Sawyer needed a moment to absorb it without her looking at him.

"I want to get to a place where I'm ready to be married to you," she said.

Sure enough, Sawyer almost dropped the tongs so much surprise hit him in the chest. He flipped the chicken, trying to find something to say. In the end, he closed the grill and looked at her. "I don't know what to say to that."

Because she'd just admitted she wasn't in that place right now. And hadn't been, even when she'd been staying over with him for those few weeks.

He felt like he'd been hollowed out with an ice cream scoop, and he could barely look at Jeri. "I think I hear the oven timer," he said, though there was no way it had been forty minutes already. Didn't matter. He had to get away from her for a minute. Just until he collected his thoughts.

Just for a couple of months.

Their make-believe marriage agreement mocked him as he practically sprinted up the steps and into his cabin, not even bothering to close the door behind him. He passed the oven, which didn't have a timer going off, and continued into his bedroom, where he closed and locked the door.

His chest heaved, and he tried to figure out why he was so upset. So angry.

"Because everything Jeri's done feels...fake," he said, his fury frothing along with foolishness and absolute humiliation.

Chapter Seventeen

Jeri worked in the kitchen at Karla's, doing exactly what the marketing executive told her to. She'd spent some time with the other woman over the past couple of months since she'd first talked to her about the cabins, and she wasn't as stiff as Jeri had first judged her to be.

Emotion choked her, but she kept stirring the custard in the pot, just like Karla had told her to. It wasn't quite custard yet, but when the cream boiled, they'd put in egg yolks and cook it into a fine pudding. At least that was what Karla had said.

"So he didn't come out of the bedroom?" Karla asked, stepping next to Jeri at the stove to pour a container of half and half into a second pot.

Jeri shook her head. She'd taken the stuffing out of the oven and rapped on Sawyer's bedroom door. He'd called that he wasn't well and for her to leave, and she'd seen no other choice.

So she'd left—just like she had when Howie had asked her to, all those years ago.

"What are you going to do?"

"I don't know," she said. She'd lain awake for hours last night, trying to find a solution to her problem. Sawyer hadn't been home when she'd woken, and while she knew she could find him somewhere on the ranch, she'd needed to come to Karla's to help with the Thanksgiving Day dinner preparations.

She was glad she wasn't at the homestead with Scarlett, Amber, and Sissy, as they were more gossipy than Karla, who only wore concern on her face.

"I've hurt him," she said. "He loves me, and I...don't love him. Now he knows it."

"Of course you love him," Karla said. "I've seen you two together, and you love him."

"Not the way he loves me," Jeri said, knowing the difference between loving someone and being *in* love with them. "I love him because he helped me when I had no one else. Because he's hard-working, and has a good heart, and listens to his gut." She shook her head again, noticing the milk starting to bubble. "This is ready for the eggs."

"Okay, we have to temper them." She turned around and collected the bowl of egg yolks she'd whisked together with sugar. "Ladle a little in here, and I'll stir them."

Jeri did as she was told, saying, "I basically told him I

wasn't in a place where I could be married to him. And yet —" Her hands shook, and Karla poured the eggs in the pot and passed her the whisk.

"Whisk," she said. "Two more minutes." She moved back over to her pot and put three bags of sweet corn into the pot. "And yet what?"

"I *was* married to him. Did things only married people do."

"Oh," Karla said.

"I'm a horrible person," Jeri said, letting her tears out now, because the way she whisked the eggs like they'd done her a personal wrong wasn't bleeding out the negativity in her life.

"Maybe you just need to get a few things fixed," Karla said. "Remember how I walked in that administration building last week and was like, 'This whole place needs to be bulldozed,' and you said, 'No, the bones are great.'? Remember?"

Jeri nodded, sniffling. "I remember."

"Well, maybe you and Sawyer have the bones of a good relationship. Maybe you just need to knock down a wall, or put in a new door, or something." Karla looked at her with earnestness. "I don't know. I'm just making all that up. I don't know construction."

Jeri half-laughed and half-cried. "Thank you, Karla."

She let the other woman take her into a quick hug before Karla said, "Oh, goodness. This is going to be a thick pudding. Pull it off the heat, Jeri. Quick."

She continued to help with the pies Karla had been assigned for the meal, wishing she could turn the clock back so lunchtime would never come.

But come it did, and Jeri joined everyone in the homestead, where Scarlett was directing Hudson where to move the furniture so he and Sawyer could set up the tables they needed to feed everyone.

Jeri met Sawyer's eye, but he looked away quickly.

She knew she wasn't as good as him, and guilt mingled with embarrassment inside her. She wanted to leave, but she had nowhere else to go. She loved this ranch, but the thought also made her angry.

Hadn't her love for this ranch been what had gotten her in trouble?

No, she told herself. *Your choices were what got you here.*

Another glance at Sawyer reminded her how much she cared about him, and how empty her life had been without him. Those few days a couple of weeks ago where she didn't go to his cabin in the evening had been terrible for her.

She'd known then that she wanted him in her life long-term. But she'd also realized that she wasn't ready for such a commitment, not without some serious attitude shifts.

In the resulting days, she'd struggled mightily with God to learn what she needed to do in order to get that attitude toward marriage and family to a place where she could see she and Sawyer as husband and wife—and maybe a family.

She'd finally come to the conclusion that she needed to

go all the way back to her first marriage and family. The origin of all of her opinions about such things.

Thus, the trip to Eugene. She hadn't been able to articulate all of that to Sawyer, and what she had said had turned out terribly.

Looking around at everyone gathered for a meal to express their gratitude, Jeri wanted to do the same.

Thank you, she prayed silently. *Please help me do what's right.*

She realized now she should've been praying for that all this time, but she'd been so focused on rebuilding what she'd lost. So focused on herself.

"All right," Scarlett said, trying to talk above all the chatter. "All right."

Hudson put his fingers in his mouth and whistled, which got everyone to be quiet. He looked at her, smiled, and nodded as if to say, *Go ahead, sweetheart.* She beamed back at him with such love in her eyes.

Again, Jeri marveled at their love—and she desperately wanted it for herself. She looked at Sawyer again, but he stood in the kitchen with Cache, Dave, and Lance, his eyes trained on Scarlett.

So she'd make things right with Howie and Randy, and then she'd see if her heart had any open doors for Sawyer.

She sure hoped it would.

Please, she prayed this time, not able to add anything else to her plea to the Lord.

Chapter Eighteen

Sawyer understood now why Carson had left the ranch. Being in the same room with Jeri was an exquisite form of torture that took his appetite from him and made his mood surly. He stayed in the kitchen with his new friends, trying not to gnash his teeth while he listened to Scarlett thank them all for being there.

"The ranch couldn't be what it is without all of you." She gazed around at them, so much gratitude oozing from her that Sawyer could feel it way down in his toes. He was grateful for *her*, that she'd come to this failing ranch and revived it when he and Gramps hadn't been able to do the same.

"So let's eat," she said. "I know Adele's not here, and she would've done such a better job than I did. But we managed to get a couple of turkeys done, mashed potatoes, gravy...." She continued listing off the food, as if everyone couldn't figure out what each pan or bowl held. "And Karla made pies."

"Jeri helped," Karla said, stepping next to Scarlett. Sawyer looked at Jeri, the way everyone else did. She smiled and stood off to the side, and Sawyer glanced away, once again angry that his heart pulsed for her. Only her. Why had he allowed himself to fall in love with her? Kiss her? Make love to her?

He'd known their relationship was on fragile ground— make-believe ground. Pretend, fake, not-really-there ground. He'd known it, and he hadn't acknowledged it, because he didn't want it to be true.

He swallowed hard, his throat so dry and his humiliation rising up to choke him. He had to get out of this house. Away from this ranch. From her.

Scarlett said, "Let's eat," and chaos erupted. Since he was in the kitchen, if he didn't go through the line and get out of the way, he'd be clogging the limited space. And everyone would pass by him, including Jeri. So while he didn't really want to eat, and he certainly didn't want to be one of the first, he got in line behind Cache anyway.

"You okay?" the other cowboy asked him, glancing over his shoulder.

"Fine," Sawyer said, not willing to talk about anything of importance right now, in front of all these people. There were at least twenty people here—anyone who didn't have somewhere else to go. Cowboys and volunteers alike. He did have somewhere else to go, but he hadn't wanted to make the two-hour drive to his parents' in Newport and show up unannounced—and alone.

There would be so many questions, his mind spun just thinking about it. So he put turkey and potatoes and stuffing on his plate and got out of the kitchen. He took a seat at the very end of the table beside Cache, with Dave and Lance across from them. They talked about their music and the band, and Sawyer could handle that. Sort of. He was still a bit stung they hadn't asked him to be in their little group, but at least he didn't have to look at Jeri or talk about Jeri.

"So Sawyer," Cache said, twisting toward him slightly. "We wanted to ask you to be in the band."

"What?" Sawyer looked at him and then the other two cowboys. "Are you serious?"

Cache grinned and nodded. "Yeah, you're good, and we'd love to have you."

"Yeah," Dave said. "Cache said you played guitar, but you were so busy with Jeri...." He trailed off and cleared his throat. "What do you think?"

"I'm in," Sawyer said, a smile touching his face that felt real and good.

"Awesome," Dave said.

"We're practicing this afternoon," Cache added. "So don't load up on turkey and then fall asleep."

They all laughed, and Sawyer couldn't wait to tell—

His good mood evaporated with the fact that he didn't have anyone to share his good news with. Not anymore.

He kept the smile on his face, though, wondering if it was as hard for Jeri as it was for him. She'd told him that she'd learned to smile through any situation, and he stole a glance at her.

She sat far away, practically as far from him as she could, Karla on one side of her and Amber on the other. Her back faced him, and she didn't seem to be bothered that he was in the same room with her.

Maybe he could stay here and live next door to her and not have her. The idea felt completely wrong, and yet he didn't have anywhere else to go.

After lunch and before band practice, Sawyer loaded Blue in the back of his truck and went down the road to town. He drove around a bit, glad for the sunshine and the breeze. He somehow ended up at the gray brick building where he went to church, and he parked and got out.

"C'mon, Blue," he said to the dog, who jumped out of the back and trotted over to the grass to sniff around. Sawyer started walking down the path that circled the bluff, thinking of Jeri up on it, on the ranch.

"What do I do about her?" he asked the Lord. He drew in a deep breath, trying to find his center. Not much came to mind, and his gut certainly didn't settle. The ache there could've been from the huge serving of sweet potato casserole he'd eaten, but he somehow didn't think so.

He continued to walk, letting Blue roam and explore, until he had to get back to the ranch for band practice. As he whistled to Blue to come back, Sawyer had the distinct thought that he should go see Gramps.

For so long, it had just been him and Gramps on the ranch. Sawyer had done everything he could for the large animals, and he'd checked on Gramps's work with the cats and dogs once a week to make sure they were getting cared for.

They'd struggled. They'd spent evenings together. He'd listened to Gramps tell stories of his wife, stories about his kids, stories about the ranch, stories about his grandkids. He realized that since he'd started seeing Jeri, he'd stopped visiting Gramps.

His truck came back into view, and Sawyer resolved to get over to Gramps's cabin before the sun set that night.

But first, he had his very first official practice with the Last Chance Cowboys, and he couldn't miss that.

SAWYER DIDN'T GO SEE Gramps that night. Or the next. Or the next. Something always came up, and the thought faded to the back of his mind, where it hung out. It only poked him at the most inconvenient times, when he couldn't drop everything and go find the old man.

After all, he couldn't call Gramps at ten o'clock at night, when the thought suddenly came forward as Sawyer went to bed. Or in the middle of holding a horse so Cache could shoe it. Or out on the range while he mapped out their agriculture plan for the next year with Jackson, a new cowboy

Scarlett had hired to oversee all the farming and feeding needs on the ranch.

Days passed and became a week. Sawyer kept himself busy in new ways now that Jeri stayed away in the evenings again. In fact, sometimes her car was gone when he got home, and he'd never finished work before her in the past.

He wondered where she was going, but he didn't ask. He got up earlier so his morning routine of sipping coffee on the porch was over before she walked by. Sometimes, in a moment of weakness, he stood at the window and watched for her to walk by.

She always looked up to his steps, and a button of hope pinned itself to his heart. Maybe she would come back to him. Maybe she'd find a way to accept that she could trust him and that they could build a strong, real marriage out of this mess.

Then he'd remind himself that she didn't want a family, and he never could get past that sticky point.

One morning close to Christmas, he still sat on his porch when her front door opened. He almost jumped to his feet and darted inside, but something told him to stay very still. So he did, watching as she brought a suitcase down her steps and put it in the trunk of her car.

She didn't glance his way as she got behind the wheel, and she pulled out and went around the U toward the other road, the one that didn't pass directly in front of his house. He watched the dust lift into the air behind her tires, watched her drive away from the ranch, from him.

"Good luck, sweetheart," he whispered to her, hoping the Lord would somehow, some way, help her with whatever she felt like she had to do in Eugene. Part of him wanted to be with her, but another part understood that she had some demons in her past she had to face herself.

All he could do now was pray that she'd be strong enough to defeat them, and that she'd hurry back to the ranch—and him.

Sighing, he decided that this morning would be a perfect time to finally go see Gramps. It wouldn't be too early, as the old man had often told Sawyer he got up at four-thirty every morning. When Sawyer had asked him why, Gramps had claimed it was just his old body completing an old habit.

Sawyer took Blue, as Gramps's second love on this Earth behind his late wife was a dog. Any dog. Didn't even have to be a good one, though Blue was the best.

"We're goin' to see Gramps," he said. "It's been a while, so don't go all nuts when you see him."

Past the homestead and across the lawn, Blue stayed right next to Sawyer, who finally rapped lightly on Gramps's door.

"It's open," the man called from inside, and Sawyer twisted the doorknob.

"Hey, Gramps," he said, entering the cabin. Gramps had a bit of a hoarding problem, but Scarlett had helped him clean out a lot of stuff. There were still piles on almost every surface, and the scent of old newspaper mixed with the slight odor of spoiled milk.

"Sawyer," he said, pushing himself out of his recliner with a groan. "And Blue." He grinned as he bent over to pat the dog. Blue had forgotten Sawyer's lecture about not going nuts, and his whole body wagged as Gramps tried to stroke him with his shaking hands. He chuckled, his voice rusty, and then he trained his watery blue eyes on Sawyer.

"It's been a while."

"Yeah," Sawyer said, following Blue and bending to give the old man a hug. "Things have been crazy around here."

"So I've heard." Gramps stutter-stepped into the kitchen. "I've got coffee."

"Sure," Sawyer said, though he didn't need more caffeine. He'd learned when he'd first come to the ranch not to refuse coffee from Gramps—it had actually been Grams who'd made it back then.

He'd tried, and they'd insisted so vehemently, that he'd given in. That was just how it was with them. Sawyer breathed in deeply, the memories of his time here sweet and sad and everything in between.

He supposed that was what life was. Sweet and sad and everything in between. "How've you been?" he asked, accepting the mug from Gramps. "Scarlett still letting you feed the dogs?"

"Oh, she's got people for everything now," Gramps said, somewhat huffily, as he collapsed back into his recliner. "That Genevieve lets me into the yard, but she doesn't leave me alone for long."

Sawyer grinned, recalling a fire Gramps had started not

that long ago, before Genevieve had come to the ranch to oversee the quality of care in the Canine Club. "Well, at least you can still get in."

"Right? It's like I've never fed a dog before." He scoffed and waved one wrinkled hand. "Anyway, that's about all I do these days. My bones hurt all the time."

Concern ran through Sawyer. "They do? Have you told Scarlett?"

"Oh, she's busy," Gramps said. "Her wedding is just a few months off, and I'm fine."

"I haven't seen you around the ranch," Sawyer said.

"I go for a walk every day," Gramps said. "Blue usually finds me."

"Does he?" Sawyer didn't know that, but it was true that Blue didn't stay by his side all day while he worked.

"And I've been assigned to get the eggs from that new coop," he said with a hint of pride in his voice. "Those two things about do me in." He laughed again, the sound morphing into a cough that once again sent worry through Sawyer.

He thought about the chores he had to do that day, and his bones started to ache too. "Well, I—"

"Heard you got hitched," Gramps said, those eyes sharp now and hooking right into Sawyer.

"Well, kind of," Sawyer said.

"I didn't get invited?" Gramps asked.

No one had been invited, but Sawyer didn't say that. "It was a spur of the moment thing."

"And where is Jeri?"

"Um, Eugene."

He nodded as if Sawyer had indeed given the right answer. "Why didn't you go with her?" Gramps seemed to know all the answers to his questions, and Sawyer squirmed on the couch.

"Honestly, Gramps, we're not together anymore," Sawyer said. "She filed for divorce and everything."

Surprise lit Gramps's face, and Sawyer realized that not all the news had circulated around the ranch yet. Sure, Cache, Dave, and Lance knew he and Jeri had broken up. Surely Scarlett, Amber, Karla, and Sissy did too. Everyone probably did. Heck, even Genevieve who didn't live on the ranch full-time had known he and Jeri were married.

But maybe they hadn't known she'd filed for divorce.

"It takes six months to go through," Sawyer said, clearing his throat afterward.

"So is she gone for good?"

"I hope not," Sawyer said.

Gramps cocked his head and looked at Sawyer. "You're still in love with her."

Sawyer wanted to leave. Grow wings and fly away, anything so he didn't have to have this conversation. Didn't have to admit to anything.

"Love is a powerful thing," he said. "Did I ever tell you how Janice and I met?"

"No, sir," Sawyer said. He'd heard a lot of stories, but not that one.

"There was a dance," he said. "She was on the committee for it, and the first time I saw her, she was halfway up a ladder, trying to get the end of a banner to stick to the wall." He wore such a look of bliss on his face, Sawyer could almost imagine the scene before him.

"I was in my Navy uniform, and I was shipping out in the morning. But I had to know who she was. I hurried over to help her, and we talked and danced all night. I kissed her that night."

"Gramps," Sawyer said with a smile. "Don't you know you're not supposed to kiss and tell?"

He chuckled. "Times were different then, I suppose. Anyway." He took a big breath and continued. "I left the next morning, and we wrote to each other. It was hard to get mail on the ship, so I'd usually get four or five letters at once, and send her several back with the mail delivery copter. When I got back to California, I looked her up. I hadn't heard from her in a while."

"Oh?" Sawyer asked, more interested in this story than he probably should've been. He had pigs to feed and cows to check on and surely Cache would be wondering where he was by now. But he leaned forward and watched the love and happiness roll across Gramps's face.

"She was dating someone else," he said, a frown marring his expression. "I told her we were meant for each other, and I don't know why, but she agreed." He shook his head and chuckled. "We were married a few weeks later, right before I had to ship out again."

"Wow," Sawyer said. "So you didn't see each other much."

"No," Gramps said. "And when I got back from that tour, my service was over. I left the Navy, and we came up here to this ranch. Been here ever since."

"And you were happy here?" Sawyer asked, though he knew the answer to that question.

"There were a lot of hard times," Gramps said, his voice choking. "The first couple of years we were here, living together and trying to build a life—so hard. I realized then that I barely knew her, and she barely knew me, and some days all we had were the memories that we loved each other. Somehow, we stayed together and made things work."

Sawyer nodded, his phone buzzing in his back pocket. "That's an amazing story, Gramps."

"It's not just a story, son," he said as Sawyer pulled out his phone to see who'd texted. "It's called real life."

Cache had asked Sawyer where he was, and he stood up. "I have to run, Gramps. One of the other cowboys is lookin' for me."

Gramps got up too and hobbled with Sawyer to the front door of the cabin. "Thanks for stopping by," he said.

"Of course," Sawyer said. "I'll be back sooner next time."

Gramps held open the door and said, "Looks like Blue's gonna stay with me."

"You keep 'im," Sawyer said with a smile.

"I hope you figure things out with Jeri," Gramps called, and Sawyer lifted his arm in a wave.

He didn't think he and Jeri could do what Gramps and Grams had done. Sure, maybe they'd both gotten married too early, but Grams had obviously loved Gramps as much as he'd loved her, and well, that just wasn't the case with Jeri.

Sawyer could love her with his whole heart and soul, but if she didn't feel the same about him....

He pushed the thoughts away as he rounded the homestead to find Cache waiting in his idling truck so they could head down to the farm supply store for the supplies they needed to build a new fence around a new pasture for the cattle.

"There you are," Cache said as Sawyer opened the passenger door and got in.

"Here I am," he said. "Let's go."

Chapter Nineteen

Rain met Jeri when she got off the plane. She knew nobody else would be waiting for her, so she said hello to the drizzle under her breath, collected her bag from the overhead compartment, and made her way through the airport to the taxi line.

Her heart skipped every other beat, though she hadn't even contacted Howie or Randy yet. She had a week here in Eugene, and she was feeling more and more foolish for coming without telling anyone.

Her problems couldn't be fixed in a week—especially when the two men she needed to see didn't even know she was in town.

She stepped to the front of the taxi line and gave the man the address to the hotel she'd booked. She had two more months on the project at Last Chance Ranch, and she'd still done nothing to find another job. She'd put in no bids, she hadn't incorporated her construction business again, none of it.

Jeri felt completely lost, adrift at sea, and she was desperately trying to find a life preserver somewhere.

She knew who she wanted to latch onto—Sawyer Smith —but she hadn't dared go see him over the past few weeks. Since that disastrous night where she'd admitted she wasn't ready for a relationship, let alone a marriage, and she'd been participating in both.

"Here you go," the man said, handing the slip of paper with the address to her driver. He took her bag and loaded it into the trunk of the cab, and she slid into the backseat.

He drove through the rain to the appointed place and Jeri went inside to see if she could check-in early. She couldn't, but they would keep her suitcase for a few hours until check-in arrived.

With nowhere to go and nothing to do, she pulled in a deep breath and pulled out her phone. She had a phone number for Howie, but whether it was the right one or not, she wasn't sure. She had one for Randy too, and she was fairly certain it was the right one, though he'd never answered one of her calls, nor returned any of her messages.

She tried Howie first, because, in the past, he'd at least picked up when she'd called. The phone rang once, twice, three times, and her heartbeat felt like it was trying to attack her.

He finally said, "Jeri?" his voice sounding tinny and far away.

"Hello, Howie," she said, not quite sure what else to add.

"What's going on?" he asked, his voice getting louder now.

"Look, this might sound strange, but I'm in town, and I need to see you."

"You're in Eugene?" His shock could not have been higher, and it ignited a fire under Jeri's mood.

"Yes," she said strongly. "And I'd like to see you as soon as possible."

"It's the holidays, Jeri. We're busy."

"I can meet for lunch. Thirty minutes."

Howie sighed like she'd inconvenienced him greatly. Maybe she had. Guilt flowed through her, but she pushed it back. She couldn't move forward with Sawyer unless she resolved this part of her past with Howie.

"Fine," he said. "I work downtown. I'll text you the address. We can meet at twelve-thirty."

"Thank you, Howie," she said, pure relief in the words. He said nothing else, and the call ended. A few moments later, her phone chimed with the address, and Jeri hurried back inside the hotel to have the receptionist help her get a cab.

At twelve-thirty, she stood in the lobby of the appointed building, ignoring the daggered looks of the security guard a dozen feet away. She wasn't the only one loitering about, but she didn't wear a lanyard around her neck like everyone else. If Howie didn't show up in the next—

"Hello, Jeri," a man said, and Jeri turned toward her ex-husband. He looked good, all dressed up in slacks, a white shirt, and a gold and yellow checkered tie.

"Howie," she said.

"What's this about?" he asked, making no move toward the door. He wasn't wearing a jacket, and he didn't carry an umbrella.

Jeri wasn't sure what it was about, and her thoughts felt like a cyclone in her brain. Finally, she said, "Randy."

"I can't control him, Jeri," Howie said with a long, exaggerated sigh. "He's a grown man, and if he doesn't want to talk to you, I can't help that." He barely looked at her, instead scanning the lobby for someone more important.

Oh, but he could. Anger simmered in Jeri's veins, but she hadn't flown here to argue with her ex. "I shouldn't have walked away," she said. "You shouldn't have asked me to walk away."

Howie lasered in on her. His eyes stormed with fury she thought he'd unleash. He'd said plenty of unkind things to her in the past. Then, as if someone had flipped a switch, he softened. "I know," he said. "I was wrong about that."

Jeri blinked, as she hadn't been anticipating an apology. Technically, Howie hadn't apologized yet, but he'd never admitted he was wrong before either.

"I'd like to see him," she said. "I—" She didn't want to

tell Howie anything about Sawyer or the stupid things she'd done these past five months. He didn't get to pull up a chair at her table and know everything after all this time.

"I've met someone," she said carefully. "And he wants a family, and I don't even know what that looks like. You...." She shook her head, her emotions getting the better of her. She fought against them, looking out the window at the rain sluicing down.

"I'll call him," Howie said, falling back a step. "Give me a minute." He turned and walked away from her, pulling his phone out of his pocket and lifting it to his ear.

Jeri stared at his shoulders, the way he still gestured with his left hand while he talked on the phone. He worked in a building that had law offices and corporate offices, and she knew he'd made something of himself, just like he'd always claimed he would.

His life here was vastly different than the one she lived at Last Chance Ranch, and as she stood in the busy building, with men and women coming in and out, she felt very much alone. Very different.

And absolutely wonderful. She didn't want this life any more than he'd want her ranch one. And that was okay. *She* was okay.

Howie glanced over his shoulder, his eyes cutting into Jeri's. She moved forward without him doing anything. When she reached his side, he extended the phone to her. "He wants to talk to you."

Jeri took the phone, feeling like it might be a trick. A

trap. A poisonous snake that would rear up and bite her the moment she put it to her ear.

"I'm sorry," he said to her, but she wasn't sure what he was sorry about. He walked away, leaving her to speak to her son.

Her son.

A person she hadn't spoken to in eight years.

She lifted the phone to her ear, and asked, "Randy?"

"Mom," he said, and Jeri burst into tears. Words bubbled out of her then, apologies for walking away all those years ago, for not trying harder to see him, for not fighting for him.

"Mom," he said again. "It's okay. Just calm down."

But it wasn't okay, and Jeri didn't know how to deal with this fury of emotions inside her. She'd known they were there, but it was easier to drive a nail into wood, or write up a new bid, or hire a plumber for a big job than it was to deal with them.

"Let's talk tonight," her son said. "I'm in the middle of something right now."

"What are you doing?" she asked.

"I'm on a build, and I've got my building inspector here. Please, I'll call you later."

Just like that, he was gone as fast as she'd gotten him back. As if Howie had been listening to her conversation and knew it was over, he turned back to her. She lowered the phone the words, *I'm on a build* in her ears.

He approached, a bit of trepidation on his face. "Well?"

"Well," she repeated, thrusting his device back at him as

her anger exploded again. "He works in construction. Why didn't you tell me that?"

Howie swallowed. "I don't know."

"You've kept him from me for fifteen years," Jeri said, her fury mushrooming up into a huge cloud that obscured her thoughts. "I can't believe you would do that. I've been nothing but nice to you from the moment we met. I *married* you so you wouldn't be humiliated in front of your friends. I supported you through law school. I—"

"I know," Howie said, grabbing onto her arm. "Can we go outside, please?"

Jeri wrenched her arm away from him, everything happening so fast. She needed to slow down. Calm down.

Mom.

It's okay, Mom.

She turned without another word and marched toward the exit. It was too loud in the lobby to know if Howie was following her or not, and when Jeri burst out into the rain, she tilted her head toward the heavens and let the water wash down her face.

"Help me forgive him," she prayed right out loud, an umbrella opening above her a moment later.

"There's a coffee shop down the street," Howie said. "We can talk there."

"I don't want to go," she said, facing him under the small space of protection from the rain.

"I'm sorry, Jeri," he said. "I knew the second I asked you to leave us alone, to let me raise him by myself, that I was wrong." He had to speak loudly to be heard above the sound of rain against the umbrella.

"Why didn't you tell me then?" she asked. "We could've been a family."

He shook his head. "No, Jeri. You didn't love me. I knew it. I couldn't stand to be so close to you when I knew that." Sadness overcame him, and he looked away. "I thought I was doing the right thing. Cutting you loose. Letting you go, to live your own life, pursue your own dreams. Do all the things you would've done had you not been the one standing beside me that night."

She stared out into the rain too, wishing she could turn back time and spend time building the right things in her life—her relationship with her son—instead of a business and buildings for other people.

"You shouldn't have been saddled by me, and by the son I gave you." He touched her shoulder, and she looked at him. "I thought I was doing the right thing. When he'd ask me about you, I told him what you did. I showed him your website. All of it."

Jeri didn't believe him. "Why didn't he want to talk to me, then? Why wouldn't he answer my phone calls on his birthday?" She'd tried. Maybe not as hard as she should've. There was so much more she could've done.

"You can ask him that tonight," he said. "He shut me out a long time ago too."

"He did?"

Howie pressed his mouth together into a thin line and

nodded. His eyes stormed as hard as Mother Nature currently was when he looked at her again. "We're not even getting together for the holidays. He has a girlfriend, and she's more important to him than I am."

Despite what Howie had done, Jeri wanted to console him. Something passed between them while they stood in the rain, and Jeri recognized the feeling. It was the same one that she'd had as she'd stood across from him in front of the altar all those years ago. The same one she'd had when Sawyer had helped her.

Understanding. Acceptance. Forgiveness.

She nodded, said, "Thank you, Howie," and stepped out from under the umbrella and into the rain.

Chapter Twenty

Sawyer pushed against the hind end of a stubborn dairy cow, disgusted that Cache preferred cattle to horses. They were so stubborn, and he couldn't get them to load onto the trailer to save his life.

Cache walked up behind him and said, "Let's go, cow," before slapping it on the rump. The cow moved, almost sending Sawyer to the ground face-first.

"I hate this," Sawyer complained as he caught himself. "How did you do that?"

"Magic cattle touch." Cache grinned at him like he was having the time of his life. As Sawyer had gotten to know the other cowboys in the band, he realized that Cache was a lot like Jeri—very sunny outlook on life.

Dave dated everyone of the opposite gender that he could—except Sissy Longston. Despite telling Sawyer that he was fine by himself, he went out with everyone from Amber to Karla to any female volunteer he could chat up enough to ask.

Everyone on the ranch could see that he liked Sissy, but he'd steadfastly said he didn't, and he wouldn't go out with her.

Sawyer didn't care who he went out with, and he didn't see Sissy all that much. She worked out of a room in the adoption center, because the administration buildings were all abandoned and in need of repair.

He'd worked through the morning to get the new cattle pasture fenced and ready, and now, if he and Cache could just get these last few cows loaded up, they could move them and go home for the night.

Sawyer turned and nearly got ran over by two more cows that Cache had magicked up the ramp to the trailer. He hopped down before he became ground beef himself and glanced toward the homestead to see Scarlett coming toward him.

She wore a cowgirl hat and lifted her palm to the top of her head to keep it seated as the wind tried to steal it away. Instantly, he knew he was the one she wanted to talk to. How he knew, he wasn't sure.

A single cow had escaped the formation Cache had put them in, and Sawyer started toward the far corner of the pasture to retrieve the cow. If Scarlett wanted to talk to him, she could, but he had work to do and it had been a long day already.

"Come on, cow," he said to the animal, moving around behind it so it would move toward the trailer. He stayed close to the fence, driving the cow in toward the trailer.

Cache saw him and came to help, saying, "He's the last one."

Working together while Scarlett watched, Sawyer and Cache got the errant dairy cow into the trailer, and Cache bolted the door.

"Nice," he said, knuckle-bumping Sawyer like they were fifteen years old. "I think the boss wants to talk to you."

"Do we have a minute?" Sawyer asked, eyeing Scarlett with her right foot up casually on the bottom rung of the fence.

"Sure," Cache said, obviously not as tired as Sawyer. He clearly slept at night instead of obsessing over a certain brunette and how he could get her back.

"What's up, Scarlett?" Sawyer asked as he approached the woman.

"Did you know Jeri went to Oregon?"

Sawyer sighed and looked toward the road leading off the ranch. "Yeah, I knew."

"Why didn't you go with her?"

He swung his gaze back to her, aware that Cache stood only a few feet away, also watching. "She didn't invite me."

Scarlett blew out her breath and looked left and then right too. "Do you know if she's planning on putting in a bid on the administration building project?"

She'd talked about it back in November, when they were

still talking to one another. Before she'd told him she wasn't ready to let him into her life.

"I thought so," he said with a frown. "She hasn't?"

"No, and they're due by next week. If she doesn't bid, Forever Friends won't let me hire her."

"Have you called her?"

"She's not picking up."

Words stormed through Sawyer's soul. Truths and facts that were not his to tell. He pressed his lips together to keep them all in, wishing he could put in a bid for Jeri.

"Did you guys break up?" Scarlett asked next, and it felt like the conversation had moved from professional to personal.

"Yeah," Sawyer said, his heart heavy when he'd worked so hard all day to get it to lighten up. "She's...we're...it's complicated." He wasn't going to throw her under the bus. She didn't deserve that, even if she had ripped his heart out and left it on his front lawn to bake in the California sun.

"What's she doing in Oregon?" Cache asked, leaning against the fence too.

Sawyer glanced at him, trying to decide if he should remain quiet or tell a little white lie. He was so tired of the half-truths and trying to do what was right. His head pounded, and he said, "I know why she's there, but it's not my business to tell."

Cache nodded as he accepted his answer, and they both looked back at Scarlett. She seemed as nervous as a chicken with a coyote out. "I know why she's there too," she said, "And Sawyer, she needs you there with her."

"No," he said immediately, shaking his head. "If there's one thing I know about Jeri Bell, it's that she doesn't need me."

He hated the words as they streamed out of his mouth. Hated how true they sounded. Hated that Scarlett wore a sad look on her face and cocked her head as if to see him better.

"Her last name is Smith," she said.

"I know what her last name is," Sawyer practically barked back. "I'm not going to Eugene." He walked backward for a couple of steps. "Can we get these cows moved?" He looked desperately at Cache. "I'm starving, and I just want to go home."

"I don't know," Cache said, looking between Scarlett and Sawyer. "I think the boss wants you to go get Jeri and make sure she gets that bid in."

"That's right," Scarlett said, her face brightening.

"No," Sawyer said. "That's outside the scope of my job description." He couldn't believe Cache and Scarlett were ganging up on him. Could not believe it. Wasn't Cache supposed to be on his side?

"Do you at least know when she'll be back?" Scarlett asked. "With the holiday and everything, I'm afraid she'll miss the deadline."

Sawyer hadn't talked with her about her specific plans,

but if she was making the trip up to see her son and ex-husband, he suspected she'd be gone for several days. "My best guess is a week or so," he said.

"She'll miss the deadline." Scarlett heaved another sigh and looked toward the exit of the ranch. "Do you think *you* could call her?"

"What makes you think she'll pick up a call from me?" he asked. "We haven't spoken since Thanksgiving." His chest pinched and pitched, and he had a hard time getting a decent breath.

"She'll think it's important," Cache said. "Right, Scarlett?"

"What are you doing?" Sawyer asked his friend. "I'm not doing this." He turned and walked away from both of them, very aware of Scarlett's higher pitched voice saying something to Cache. He didn't care. He wasn't going to call Jeri, and he certainly wasn't going to go to Eugene.

He avoided the cow pies as he marched back to the trailer Cache had pulled right into the center of the field. He didn't care if he roasted to death in the cab, with the scent of manured dairy cows as the only smell. It would be better than continuing that conversation.

Thankfully, he'd barely pulled himself into the truck when Cache opened the driver's door and got behind the wheel. "Sorry," he said. "I mean, I knew you and Jeri were going through a rough patch. I didn't know you hadn't talked to her since Thanksgiving."

Sawyer grunted, just wanting to get these cows moved so he could go home. Cache drove over the bumpy pasture and out onto the flatter road. He eased past the homestead and Scarlett walking back toward it and turned left toward the llamas and the new pasture they'd spent the morning fencing.

Twenty minutes later, the dairy cows had a new field of grass to munch on, and Sawyer was on his way home. As he stood in the shower, he couldn't help think about Jeri and how things were going with her son.

Without thinking too hard about it, with his towel still wrapped around his waist, he fired off a quick text.

Thinking about you. Hope things go okay with Randy.

That was simple, he thought. It wasn't too forward, he reasoned. He *was* thinking about her, he told himself.

Then he left his phone in his bedroom while he went to get something to eat with the other cowboys and then went back to Cache's for band practice.

After all, he didn't need another vein opened when Jeri ignored him and didn't text back. He could save that bleeding for bedtime.

WHEN SAWYER RETURNED to his cabin, he let Blue out the back door while he switched on the light that his dog probably didn't need.

From somewhere in the depths of his cabin, his phone chimed, causing his heart to crash against his ribcage. No wonder he hadn't taken it with him. He'd have been a nervous wreck all night, constantly checking it even when it stayed silent.

He glanced at Blue, who seemed to be sniffing around like the spot he chose was life or death, so Sawyer left the door open a crack and went to get his phone.

He indeed had texts, and he swiped to unlock his device.

"Just one text," he muttered, tapping.

But the one text was from Jeri, and she'd said, *It went okay. Would've been better if I'd brought a bird house with me.*

His eyebrows crinkled together, his memory tugging at something from months ago. "Bird house?" he asked the empty bedroom. "What does that mean?"

Blue came up beside him, and Sawyer looked at the dog. "What does that mean?" he asked the canine, who circled and laid down at his feet. So not helpful.

The text was from a couple of hours ago too, and Sawyer wasn't sure if he could message her back now, as late as it was. He turned to go into the kitchen, his brain working overtime to decode the message.

Decode.

Code word.

He and Jeri had decided on a code word months ago, in case she needed rescuing from his mother at the beach picnic. They'd never used it that day, nor in any of the days since.

Bird house.

"She needs rescuing," he said to himself, his feet frozen to the floor in the hallway. His heart seemed to grow two sizes as it bobbed in the back of his throat.

She needed him, and she'd asked him to come in a strange way, sure. But probably the only way she could at the moment.

Sawyer spun and strode back into his bedroom. He had a suitcase around here somewhere. He could pack tonight. Get his laptop out and get an airplane ticket. Show up and... he had no idea after that.

Maybe he didn't need to know after that. Maybe he should do what he should've done all along—trust Jeri and give her the time she needed.

"All right," he said, finally locating the dusty carryon bag underneath his bed. He opened it and looked at Blue. "I'm going to be so thrashed in the morning, aren't I?"

After all, he had to pack. Get a flight. Find a dog-sitter for Blue. Explain to Scarlett.

Pack. Flight. Dog-sitter. Scarlett.

He recited the words as he stepped over to his closet, ready to do anything to get Jeri back into his life. Maybe Scarlett and Cache had planted a seed earlier that day. Maybe the Lord had softened his heart—and hers. Maybe maybe maybe.

"Thank you for prompting me to text her." He hoped

whispered prayers made it to God's ears as easily as spoken ones, because he could really use the divine help about now. "Help me to know how to help her. Bring her back to me."

Pack. Flight. Dog-sitter. Scarlett.

And then...Jeri.

Chapter Twenty-One

J eri woke early the next morning, the scent in her hotel room a bit...off. Something like too much mold or mildew, though her room had been spotless when she'd checked-in. Her phone sat on the nightstand, no flashing lights in sight.

Sawyer hadn't texted back.

Her whole soul felt heavy, despite the great conversation with Randy last night.

"I wouldn't call it *great*," she muttered to herself as she went to get in the shower. They'd embraced, sure. He was all grown up, and her social media stalking of her son hadn't done justice to seeing him in person.

He was so tall, like his father, but he had her eyes, her nose, and her quick wit and fiery spirit. At least she liked to think he did.

Their conversation was stilted at best, and he kept

letting his phone interrupt him. About the time Jeri was going to declare the whole thing a mistake and excuse herself, Sawyer's text had come in.

Randy had asked about it, and she'd spent several minutes talking about Sawyer and her life at Last Chance Ranch. Everything had improved from there. Randy opened up about school, where he was studying business management and construction management. His end goal was to be a general contractor, and Jeri's whole heart felt like it had been injected with life again.

She told him about her own business, but Randy hadn't seemed that impressed. He'd gone sort of distant during the few minutes she spoke of what she'd spent her life doing, and she realized now that he probably thought she'd chosen her career over him.

Out of the shower, she couldn't remember if she'd washed her hair. There was so much going on, and she needed someone to help shoulder this load.

Not just someone.

Sawyer.

Why hadn't he texted back last night? She'd responded immediately, and unless he'd flipped his phone over and walked away from it, he should've seen it. Heard it. Something.

Her frustration coiled through her again, ready to strike.

She drew in a deep breath and looked at herself in the steamy hotel mirror. "Focus," she whispered. "One thing at a time."

She didn't need to see Howie again. Something had healed between them when he'd apologized and admitted he was wrong. She'd done plenty wrong too, but she knew how to inspect a building, make sure all the pipes went to all the right places, how to make sure the foundation and walls were strong and tight.

Yes, she and Randy were broken down. Abandoned. A bit tarnished. But just like she'd told Karla about the administration building, the bones were good.

At least she hoped they were. He'd invited her to lunch with his girlfriend that day, and Jeri had readily agreed to go. He hadn't said much about her the previous night, and she knew why. She'd been gone for a long time, and she didn't get to know everything and be involved with everything right away.

There was trust to be earned. Love to develop. Friendship to cultivate.

And she had six days left.

She sighed, the burden on her shoulders almost too much to carry. But carry it, she would. She'd done some crazy things in her life, and she actually craved the slower pace at the ranch. Jeri wanted to stay there for another project, and Scarlett had texted and called all day yesterday to tell her about the bid deadline for the administration complex build.

Jeri had meant to put together a bid and submit it, but somehow, it had got lost in the emotional turmoil of the last month. But, she had a computer with her, and she could get it done this morning before lunch with her son.

She sent a quick text to Scarlett to let her know to watch for the bid to come in later that day, and she got the idea to show it to Randy during their lunch. Her soul warmed as she sat down at her laptop and began to work.

It felt good to be working toward another goal. To have another project in her sights. She didn't want to drift anymore, and she realized that was what she'd been doing for a long time—even before she and Sawyer had lost their minds and gotten married.

With the proposal nearly finished, she went downstairs to the business center in the hotel and printed it. She could easily fold the pages and tuck them into her purse, waiting for the right moment to show them to her son.

She still couldn't believe he'd agreed to see her. She hadn't been brave enough to ask him why he refused her phone calls for all those years, but Howie said he'd shut him out too. Randy definitely carried anger around with him, and all Jeri could do as she left her hotel to go meet him for lunch was pray for him.

THE CHIME on the deli's door grated against Jeri's nerves. Randy and his girlfriend were late, and Jeri's stomach was especially upset about it. It cramped and ached, like someone was digging a very large pit inside it.

Had she been stood up? Duped? Ghosted?

Abandoned.

Her heart joined the depression train, speeding up and then slowing down. And every time that stupid chime sounded and Randy didn't walk in, she wanted to storm out.

Another ten minutes passed, and Jeri had cycled through dozens of emotions. She told herself she'd leave after the next person entered, and at this very busy lunchtime, that would only be a few seconds.

Sure enough, the door chimed and a man walked in. A man that was not her son.

But a man she knew....

Surprise and fear glued her to her seat. "Sawyer." His name fell from her lips in a whisper, and she blinked, sure she wasn't seeing things right. But she had to be. After all, not a single person who'd walked through that door had been wearing a cowboy hat, and Sawyer stuck out.

Everything in the deli quieted as he first scanned the line and then the shop. She pushed to her feet without specific thought to do so. Her body seemed to be reacting by itself, her brain on a temporary vacation.

She lifted her hand. Called, "Sawyer."

Their eyes met, and though the chime sounded again, this time, it didn't bother Jeri. How long it took for Sawyer to reach her did bother her, and the fact that he didn't sweep her into his arms and kiss her bothered her a whole lot too.

He stood on the other side of the table, the noise rushing

back into her ears as she continued to stare at him. "I can't... what are you doing here?"

"You said you needed me," he said, real low, the words almost getting lost in the lunchtime chatter.

She had said that. He'd interpreted it correctly. She had no idea why she needed him, only that she did, and before she knew it, he'd stepped around the table and lifted his hand to her face.

He wiped a tear she hadn't known had spilled out and said, "It's okay, Jeri."

She shook her head. "Nothing's okay."

"Well, isn't that why you're here? To fix a few things?"

Foolishness raced through her. "I'm so sorry," she said. "I shouldn't have asked you to marry me. I shouldn't have left my son all those years ago. Everything that's happened the last few months has been wrong." She became aware she was babbling and crying, and people were starting to look at her.

Sawyer shook his head and leaned in, effectively blocking her view of the rest of the crowd in the shop. "Mistakes have been made, but the last few months of my life have been the best ones."

Jeri searched his face, trying to find any hint of untruth. She couldn't, and that almost scared her as much as being ghosted by her son. "I'm sorry, I—"

"Do you love me?" Sawyer asked, the bite of a challenge in his tone.

She'd never told him she loved him. He'd only said those

three little words to her once. She'd always believed that actions spoke louder than words, and she'd lived with Sawyer for three weeks as his wife. How could he not know?

"Jeri," he said in a freakishly calm voice. "I need to know."

She nodded, deciding to pair the action with words, so he really would know. "Yes," she said. "I love you."

He ducked his head in that adorable way, a smile touching his mouth. When he looked up at her again, new hope shone in his eyes. "I love you, too." He inched forward, though he was already pretty much crowding her personal space. "And I want to work things out. Work on us. *I'm* not walking away."

The fire in his words wasn't lost on her.

"Are you going to walk away?" he asked.

Images from her life flashed through her eyes. She'd walked away when she should've stayed—with Randy, with her family, with her business.

"No," she said, feeling strong and powerful. "I'm not going to walk away."

Sawyer smiled and swept his cowboy hat off his head, revealing that he'd gone back to his short haircut. "Can I kiss you now?"

Jeri leaned forward and kissed him, very aware of the cheer that went up in the deli. She giggled against his lips, their kiss sloppy and misaligned. He broke their connection, his smile so wide and so genuine, and turned to the shop. His fingers found hers and he squeezed. "She said she loves me," he called to the perfect strangers who happened to be eating in the deli.

The lunch crowd clapped, and Jeri couldn't help smiling back at all the grinning people she didn't know.

"Okay," Sawyer said, finally sitting down beside her at the table for four. "Let me just send a quick text...." He released her hand and pulled out his phone. A few taps, and he focused on her again. "I hope you can forgive me."

"For what?" By her count, she was the one who needed all the forgiveness.

He nodded toward the door. "I delayed them."

Randy had entered the shop, and in the three seconds it took him to scan and find them, Jeri's whole soul had come to life. She stood to receive her son, who hugged her and glanced at Sawyer.

"All good?" he asked, his voice so deep and so foreign in her ears.

"Starting," Sawyer said as Randy stepped back. "Have to start somewhere, you know?" It seemed like Sawyer was saying more than just words, but Jeri couldn't figure them out.

A pretty blonde woman stood a half-step behind Randy, and he brought her forward. "This is Pearl Stansfield," he said. "She's my girlfriend. Pearl, my mother, Jeri, and her boyfriend, Sawyer."

Pearl smiled at everyone, and Jeri's emotions couldn't be contained. She hugged the woman as if they'd be best friends by the end of lunch. They all sat down and started chatting, only pausing when the waitress came to get their sandwich orders.

Nothing was perfect by the end of the lunch hour. World peace hadn't been achieved. Her relationship with Randy wasn't completely fixed. Nor was the one with Sawyer. But the healing process has been started, and as Sawyer had said, Jeri had to start somewhere.

Chapter Twenty-Two

"He did what?" Sawyer stared out the dingy hotel window as Cache told him again that Blue had tried to eat one of Jeri's chickens. "That's so strange. He's lived next door to those chickens for months and months. I wonder what's come over him."

"I don't know," Cache said. "We got it away from him, and the bird looks like it'll be okay. I put them both in the coop with the others by the horse barn."

"Good idea," Sawyer said.

"How'd things go with Jeri?"

"Okay." He sighed. Lunch had gone great, in his opinion. But he wasn't trying to make up for fifteen lost years and heal so much hurt. "I talked to her, and she didn't walk away."

I'm not going to walk away.

Sawyer had thought *I love you* would be the best words

on earth, especially coming from Jeri's mouth. But he'd been wrong. *I'm not going to walk away* was so much better.

"We're going to dinner tonight," he said. "It's supposed to be crazy."

"Yeah, it's almost Christmas," Cache said. Other voices came through the line, and he added, "Hey, I have to go. The band's here."

"Is that Sawyer?" Dave asked, and then he was on the line. "I can't believe you left us," he said, but his voice carried humor and heart. "Our sound sucks without you."

"And our vocals are all off," Lance called.

"So make up with Jeri and get home already," Dave said while Lance and Cache laughed about something somewhere off the line.

Sawyer chuckled too. "I'm working on it," he said. The call ended, with one word stuck in Sawyer's head.

Home.

Last Chance Ranch was his home, and he wanted it to be Jeri's too. He wanted to build a life with her, and they needed to have a serious conversation about serious things.

And they would.

She was spending the afternoon with her son on his build site, and Sawyer had come to his hotel to give them some time alone. Once her son had arrived for lunch, Jeri had seemed more like the one he'd met when she'd first come to ranch. Bubbly, bright, quick to laugh. Funny, witty, flirty.

Instead of lying down and catching the nap he needed,

he dialed Scarlett instead. "Sawyer," she said. "The bid came in."

Relief poured through him. "That's great."

"I'm so glad you went up there."

He hadn't come to make sure Jeri put in a bid on the administration project, but he just said, "Me too. Listen, I have something I want to talk to you about."

"Sounds serious," she said.

"It is." He drew in a deep breath, wondering where to start. "It's about a house at Last Chance Ranch. A permanent house—not a cabin—for me and Jeri."

SAWYER WOKE to the pealing of his ringtone. The hotel room had grown dark, and panic hit him squarely in the chest. He scrambled to sit up, to find his phone before the call ended. He managed to do one of those, and only closed his fingers around his phone after it had stopped ringing.

He switched on a lamp and dialed Jeri back, still fuzzy from sleep and hoping she was still downstairs. "Hey," he said. "Sorry, I fell asleep."

"I figured," she teased. "We don't have to go out tonight."

"No, it's fine," he said, wiping his hand down his face. "I just need five minutes to get ready." At least physically, just to throw on his cowboy boots and brush his teeth. He needed more time than that to order his thoughts and get ready to have a serious conversation with Jeri.

Several minutes later, he stepped out of the elevator to find her sitting on a couch in the lobby, looking at her phone. He paused, the sight of her so wonderful and so beautiful he couldn't believe she loved him.

Him.

She wasn't pretending, and neither was he. No, she wasn't ready for marriage, which was okay. She'd started the healing process, and he still had plenty to learn about her before *he* was ready to be married to her.

"Hey, gorgeous," he said, approaching her. She got to her feet and he wrapped his arms around her. "I missed you so much." He touched his lips to hers, seeking permission. She gave it, kissing him back with the passion he needed to feel from her.

He pulled away first, knowing they were in a public place, and asked, "Ready?"

"There's a restaurant here," she said. "Doesn't look busy. Then we wouldn't have to go downtown." She nodded behind him, and Sawyer turned in that direction.

"All right." He honestly had no idea where to go for dinner. He'd told Jeri she could pick, and if this place was okay with her, it was fine with him.

They got a table easily, and though the lighting was dimmer than he'd like, he could still see her—and the gift she brought out from her purse. The box was barely larger than his hand and wrapped in festive, red paper.

"Jeri," he said. "What's that?"

"It's a present," she said with a smile, nudging it closer to him. "Go on. Open it."

"I don't have anything for you."

"Well, you still have two days." She tossed her hair over her shoulder and grinned. "Now, hurry up. The waiter will be here in a minute."

Sawyer picked up the package and ripped the paper off. Inside sat a package of guitar picks and a few pieces of paper that had been folded in half. "What's this?" He opened the pages to find music written on them. Hand-written notes and lyrics. "You wrote a song?"

"Just the beginning," she said. "I thought you and I could finish it together. Maybe the band could play it."

Warmth filled him from head to toe, and he glanced back at the words. A few seconds passed as he absorbed them and their meaning. "Jeri, this is a love song."

"It's our love song," she said, leaning forward. "And when we get married, I want the band to play it." Her eyes sparkled like stars, and Sawyer fell in love with her all over again.

He refolded the papers and put them back in the box. "Thank you." He kissed her quickly but stayed close to her. "You think you want to marry me again?"

"Yeah," she said, a tiny smile on her mouth.

"For real?"

"For real."

Sawyer settled back into his seat, and the waiter arrived to take their drink orders. Once he'd left, Sawyer cleared his throat. "Well, since we're talking about a real, long-term relationship, I think we should discuss other things that go along with that." His eyes darted all over the booth, finally landing on her.

He calmed. "Family. Housing." He held up two fingers. "I've been working on one."

"Well, seeing as how it takes two to 'work on' a family, I'm going to guess you've been doing something with the housing." At least she didn't shut him down about a family this time. And maybe it wasn't in their cards to have kids. Sawyer could deal with that.

"I'd like to stay at the ranch," he said. "I've been there forever, and I work there."

"Mm hmm," Jeri said, lifting her water to her lips almost the moment the waiter set the glass on the table.

"I talked to Scarlett this morning, and she said she'd talk to Gramps about selling me a modest piece of land, probably near the entrance, but not in the Cabin Community. After that, I just need someone to build us a house."

"Gee, I wonder where we could find someone who could do that," she said, making him chuckle.

"I'll need to see a bid," he said, grinning at her, an explosion of love hitting him when she tipped her head back and laughed. He hadn't heard that sound in so long, and it was absolutely the best sound on the planet—especially when *he* elicited it from her.

They spent the next evening with Randy, Pearl, and her

family, and Sawyer was glad for a chance to just sit back and fade away. Watching Jeri interact with her son was eye-opening, and she was strong and capable and extremely nurturing too. Sawyer knew she didn't think of herself as a good mother, but he reasoned it was only because she hadn't had the real opportunity to be one.

He could see her as his wife, the mother of his children, and he closed his eyes and thanked God for the opportunity to be at Last Chance Ranch, and that He'd guided Jeri into his life.

"Do you want to play?" someone asked, and his eyes flew open. One of Pearl's nieces stood in front of him.

"Play what?" he asked, smiling at the towheaded little girl. Jeri's daughter would never have hair that color, but the child was cute.

"Ping pong," she said. "We have a table downstairs."

"Sure," he said, scooting forward to get off the couch. "But I'm really bad at ping pong."

"You can be on my team," she said as if she won national tournaments.

He chuckled as he followed her to the steps. He turned back and caught Jeri's eye, mouthing that he was going to go downstairs and play ping pong with the kids. Their joyful yells coming up the steps told him he'd only be able to play one game, maybe two.

At the bottom of the steps, the little girl handed him the paddle. "Here you go," she said. "You just hit it back and forth." She was so matter-of-fact, as if he'd never heard of or seen ping pong before.

"You go first," he said, and she bounced the ball and hit it. It didn't go over the net, and she couldn't reach it. Sawyer collected the ball for her and handed it back. Two boys stood on the other side of the net, at least five years older than this little girl.

Sawyer suddenly felt fiercely protective of her, and he said, "You've got it."

She hit it again, and the ball went over this time. One boy scrambled to hit it back, which he did. Sawyer bumped the ball right back over, at a steep angle, and it went flying off the table.

The little girl cheered as she jumped up and down, and footsteps came toward them. Jeri arrived first, with her son and Pearl behind her. They became the audience in a rousing match between Sawyer and the two twelve-year-olds.

Lizzy hit a few balls, but it happened more out of dumb luck than anything else. Still, Sawyer gave her high five and told her how amazing she was after every play.

The game ended—they lost by two points—and the kids ran for the stairs, saying, "Time for ice cream and presents!"

"Ice cream?" Sawyer asked, looking at Pearl.

"Yeah," she said. "My mother always has cake and ice cream for our Christmas Eve present celebration."

"But it's not Christmas Eve," Jeri said, frowning. "Isn't that tomorrow?"

Sawyer sure hoped so, because he needed to find a present for Jeri, and the stores would surely be closing early.

"Yeah." Pearl shrugged and smiled. "But my brothers are going to their other families tomorrow night. So we're doing our celebration tonight." Randy took her hand and squeezed.

"Other families?" Sawyer asked, noting the tenderness between Pearl and Randy. He hoped they could hold onto it, cultivate it, and grow together.

"Yeah, you know," she said. "My brother's wife. Her family. Sasha is from here, and they're doing a dinner over there tomorrow. And Ryan is going to his girlfriend's." She looked at Randy. "We didn't have other family...until now." She looked at Jeri with a warm smile. "I've been telling him to call you, you know?"

She said "you know" a lot, but in that moment, Sawyer didn't care. Jeri looked like she might cry, and she lunged forward to hug Pearl and then Randy. Sawyer said nothing. He did nothing. He was just there, and when Jeri sat back down beside him, he took her hand and squeezed it.

She laid her head against his bicep, and he was the luckiest man in the world.

Chapter Twenty-Three

Jeri didn't care that the sun was going down. It had been doing that so early over the past couple of months, making her days shorter than she liked. She was a month behind schedule on the dog enclosures, but no one except her cared.

And she just had one last thing to do....

She bent to swipe the final square of adhesive over the waterproofing she'd laid down earlier this week. One more panel of flooring. Then the last dog enclosure in the expansion would be finished.

Done.

Well, the building inspector was scheduled to come out tomorrow morning, and once they got his final approval, dogs could be sheltered here. Oh, and Lance needed to rework the fencing, so this enclosure would be included in the huge dog run and roaming land that took up a large part of the north end of the ranch.

She fitted the last piece of flooring into place and set it. "There." Stepping back, she felt a keen sense of accomplishment and loss at the same time.

Finishing a project was a huge deal. She celebrated every time she did, and that night, she and Sawyer had movie tickets and dinner plans. Neither of them had said anything about their marriage, impending divorce, or living together. She lived in her cabin, he lived in his.

She kissed him good morning and good-night—and every time she went down into Pasadena to see a marriage and family counselor. Which was so strange to her. She wasn't married—not really—and she didn't have a family. Not really.

Yes, she and Randy texted every day now. He was a brilliant man, with a brilliant mind, and while she wanted to support him in whatever he wanted to do, she'd asked him why construction. When he could literally do anything, why had he chosen that.

"Because you do it, Mom," he'd told her. She still warmed every time she thought about it. As if summoned by her thoughts, her phone dinged, and she looked at it to see a text from her son.

Thinking of asking Pearl to marry me. What do you think?

He'd sent messages like that over the past three months

too, and they always made Jeri smile. Instead of texting him back, she called.

"Can you talk?" she asked by way of hello.

"For a few minutes," he said.

"You're in love with Pearl?"

"I think so."

"She loves you?"

"I think so."

"You're not even twenty-one yet." Jeri let the words sit there, because they spoke all of her concerns. She could've said more, about how he had his whole life ahead of him. He could do anything, go anywhere. He hadn't finished school yet. All of it.

But she understood better than most that sometimes life didn't have to be all planned out. That life rarely went the way she wanted it to. That rash decisions—

"I just don't want you to rush into anything," she said. "When you're young, you don't have to go a hundred miles an hour."

"I haven't even been seeing her that long, either," he said. "I just...I like being with her. I figure if we like being with each other so much, what's so bad about getting married?"

"There's nothing *bad* about it," Jeri said, though she'd done it twice, both times for the wrong reasons, and she still wasn't sure there was a good reason—for her.

"You and Dad got married young," Randy said.

"Oh, honey, that wasn't even a real marriage."

"You were together for five years."

"Yeah." Jeri sighed. "But Randy, you know why we got married, right?"

Several beats of silence came through the line. "Were you pregnant with me?"

"No." She exhaled. "I can't believe your father hasn't told you this."

"He didn't talk about you much," he said. "Unless I asked and asked. Then he'd show me your website, and your picture, and talk about what you did. Buildings you worked on. That kind of thing."

Jeri had made peace with Howie's actions. She couldn't go back and change them anyway. "Well, we were out with some friends," she said. "I'd been out with your dad, oh, probably a dozen times. He was a nice guy. Smart as a whip. Worked hard in school. But, there wasn't a huge spark there. A little sizzle."

She let her mind flow back to that time. "And the guy we were with started teasing your dad. Saying how he'd never get married, never get anyone to commit to someone like him. It was quite hurtful. Anyway, to help your dad out, I stepped up and said I'd marry him. It became a contest after that, and we ended up getting married a few weeks later."

Saying it out loud sounded so, so stupid. What had she been thinking?

"I didn't get pregnant with you until a few months after that," she said. "And honestly, Randy? We stayed together as long as we did because of you."

"Why'd you leave?" Randy asked, his voice almost a whisper. She'd been anticipating this question when she'd gone to Oregon over Christmas. But he'd never asked.

"Your dad asked me to," she said simply. "He was finishing law school, and I didn't want to leave California. I'd been building my construction firm here, and we fought all the time. All the time." She swallowed, remembering those bitter days. "And he asked me to please, just let him have you, take you to Oregon, and raise you. I was weak. I walked away."

Scuffling came through the line, and he spoke to someone on his end. "Sorry," he said. "I have to go."

"Love you," she said.

"Love you too." He hung up, and Jeri looked at her phone, her mood darkening quickly.

"He still blames you for leaving," she said, picking up the tool she'd used to lay the floor. "And that's fine. He needs time to heal, just like you do."

As she loaded everything in the back of her construction truck, her phone dinged again. Randy had sent another message.

I don't blame you for walking away, Mom. I love you.

Light filled Jeri's whole being, and she felt the sweet release that only came from forgiveness. Tears filled her eyes, and she faced the heavens, with their glorious spring sunshine. "Thank you, Lord," she said. "Thank you."

A FEW WEEKS LATER, Jeri lounged in the shade near where Sawyer was working out in the pasture with the llamas. She'd won the bid for the new administration build-out, but the funding hadn't come in yet. In the time since she'd finished the dog enclosure, she'd been getting her business set up. She'd applied for her business license again and dedicated a space in her living room to business things by buying a desk and putting her paperwork there.

She'd been looking for other jobs that were bigger, and thus taking bids for items that didn't start for months and months.

She walked Blue, though the dog got more exercise than he needed just from running around the ranch. She got another chicken and kept it in the coop with the ranch hens.

She'd kept busy for the most part, but sometimes, she just hung out with Sawyer and watched the man use those glorious muscles.

Her phone rang, and she swiped on a call from Scarlett. "Did the funding come through?" she asked.

"Not yet," she said. "I'm calling for two reasons. You have an interesting piece of mail here from the State of California. And the bridesmaid dresses are here." She actually sounded more excited by the first item.

Jeri wasn't. She knew what that piece of mail held. An official notification that she and Sawyer were now divorced. Of course, maybe that was more exciting than squeezing herself into a bright blue bridesmaid dress.

"I'll come over," she said, getting up. She signaled to Sawyer and told him where she was going, and then she started down the road.

Adele would be coming back to the ranch for the wedding in just a few days, and while Jeri hadn't been besties with the woman, she'd liked her. Oh, and she made the best hamburger on the planet.

Jeri went up the steps and into the house through the back door without bothering to knock. Scarlett stood in the living room with Sissy and Amber, both of whom already had their dresses on.

"Wow," she said. "You guys look great." And they did, because they were feminine. They didn't wield hammers and hold nails between their teeth for a living. Their hands weren't chapped ninety percent of the time, with cuts and bruises the other ten percent.

Scarlett turned toward her, a huge smile on her face. "Here's yours."

"Scarlett," she said, eyeing the armful of blue fabric. "I mean, Adele will be here. You don't need me in the wedding party."

"Of course I do." Scarlett came around the couch, concern in her eyes. "Sawyer can't walk someone else down the aisle. Now come on. I need you to go put this on so I can get it altered if it needs it."

"Can you alter my hips?" Jeri joked as she took the dress from Scarlett. Everyone laughed, and Scarlett hugged her.

"Honey, if that were possible, I'd be first in line." She shooed her down the hall. "Use my bedroom. I left your mail on my dresser."

Jeri did as she was told, throwing the dress on the bed and going for the envelope that Scarlett had leaned up against her jewelry box. Her fingers trembled the tiniest bit as she tore it open and took out the letter.

Sure enough, she and Sawyer were now divorced.

She wasn't sad. Or relieved. She was just the same. At least now, she and Sawyer had the opportunity to do things the right way. A *real* way.

Moving quickly so Scarlett wouldn't get concerned and come check on her, she snapped a picture of the top part of the letter and texted it to Sawyer. *All official*, she said. *Our make-believe marriage is over.*

She then shimmied into the dress, wishing her arms weren't as big as they were. "Muscle," she told herself, though she knew her binge-eating from six to ten p.m. produced more than muscle on her frame.

A knock sounded on the door, and she said, "Come in."

Scarlett inched into the room, her eyes bright. "Are you divorced now?"

Jeri nodded, sliding her hands down her stomach and over her hips. "You know, this isn't half-bad. It's pretty flattering for us bigger girls." She smiled at Scarlett, but it felt shaky on her face.

"I love you, Jeri," she said, moving into her personal space and embracing her. "You always see the good in things. In people. In everything." She stepped back and held her at arm's length, everything moving too fast for Jeri to comprehend. "I'm sorry about the divorce."

"Me too," Jeri whispered. Then she tossed her hair and shook off the melancholy spirit. "But hey, this way, when Sawyer asks me to marry him, I can say yes. And everyone will get to come."

Scarlett wiped her eyes and looked at the opened letter and back to Jeri. "There's that silver lining again. Are you... do you think you'd say yes if he asked?"

Jeri had been seeing her counselor a lot in the past few weeks. She didn't feel like she'd had any major break-throughs. She just felt better overall. "I'm actually surprised I said that."

"I'm not," Scarlett said. "You two are made for each other."

"Like you and Hudson."

"Yeah." Scarlett smiled. "And we didn't exactly get to where we are easily either. So you and Sawyer will get there."

Jeri thought she already was, which sent comfort and peace through her. "Hey, it's easier to smile than to frown," Jeri said. "And I mean it about the dress. You did a good job picking them out."

"Thanks. Let's go show the other girls." She turned to go right as Jeri's phone went off.

"Be right there," she said, grabbing it from the dresser. Sawyer had texted back with the only thing Jeri wanted to hear.

Love you.

Chapter Twenty-Four

S awyer couldn't believe what he was about to do—alter his morning routine. The very idea felt wrong and amazing at the same time, and he pushed away any feelings he had.

Because he was running late and just needed to get things *done*.

His relationship with Jeri was stronger than ever, despite the letters they'd both received yesterday. He didn't care that he was now divorced from her—because now he could marry her for real. Invite his family, his friends, his bandmates.

And he'd been planning this proposal for a month. *Please let her be ready*, he prayed as he hurried to pour his coffee. He just wanted to sit on his front steps and sip it while the ranch woke up, his dog at his feet.

And he was going to.

On *her* front porch.

After all, she'd walked into the wrong house all those months ago. Walked right into his heart and claimed it.

She didn't have any furniture on her front porch, but Sawyer had a little table beside a chair, and he usually took his guitar out there too. Moving as quietly as he could so he wouldn't give anything away, he moved his stuff to her porch, dashing back across the lawn to get his coffee.

He went up the steps, turned, and sat, his nerves firing like a twenty-one gun salute. Cache came out on his front porch, immediately looking toward Jeri's house. His job was to distract Jeri that morning, and he grinned as he said something into the phone he had pressed against his ear.

Sawyer gave him a thumbs-up, and Cache lowered his phone a few moments later. "She's comin' now," he called.

Sawyer took another sip of coffee, the lock behind him starting to rattle. Had he even remembered the ring? He almost choked but managed to swallow his brew and pat down his pockets, satisfied when he felt the hard lump in his right one.

The door behind him opened, and it took all of his willpower not to turn toward the sound. Jeri's footsteps rushed out as she muttered something under her breath. The door slammed closed, and then she said, "Oh."

He looked up at her and took a slow sip of his coffee as he drank in her beauty—and her surprise.

"Sawyer? What are you doing here?"

"My morning routine," he said. "I always sit on the porch and drink my coffee."

She glanced toward his house, and then around her porch. "But this is *my* porch."

"Is it?" He looked at the guitar he'd leaned against the post, and the little table and chair. "Huh. Looked like mine." He patted the spot next to him. "Wanna sit for a minute?"

She looked like she did not want to sit for a minute, and Sawyer's heart thumped out too many beats at once. In the end, she did sit down next to him, a long sigh accompanying her.

"Maybe I should sit on your porch every morning," he said, taking her hand in his. "This is way better than my routine." He leaned over and kissed her, feeling her tension and frustration bleed away beneath his touch.

"I'm late," she said, but she kissed him again.

He ducked his head and took another sip of his coffee, like this was a normal, easy conversation. "Where are you going this morning?"

"Goat yoga."

He nodded. "I think Amber will understand if you're a few minutes late." He looked at her. "I wanted to ask you something."

No fear crossed her face. Her eyes stayed bright and clear as she looked at him. "All right."

"Now that we're officially divorced, I'd love it if we could tie the knot for real." He dug in his pocket and took out the diamond he'd bought a few weeks ago. "I'm in love with you, Jeri Bell, in the best way, and my loan for the house went through last week, and I didn't tell you, because I was waiting for us to be divorced, so I could ask you to marry me." He held up the ring and glanced at it. "I want you to build me a house. Live in it with me." He touched the tip of his nose to hers, feeling a slight shake coming from her. "Sit with me on the porch in the morning and kiss me good-night." He looked right into her eyes. "I want you."

He took a deep breath, having just said more than he usually did in a whole day.

"Your loan went through last week?" she asked.

"That's what you're thinking about?"

"I could've been working on the house," she said. "Instead, I've been bored out of my mind—so much so that I told Amber I'd come to *goat yoga*." She scoffed. "I don't want to go to goat yoga. I want something to *do* around here."

Sawyer blinked at her, the spark in her expression absolutely gorgeous. He burst out laughing, glad when she joined him. He started to tuck the diamond ring back into his pocket. "All right. Let's start with the house. I can get an answer—"

Her fingers curled around his wrist and squeezed. "Don't put that away," she whispered.

"Oh, you want to see this?" He closed his fist around the ring, playing a dangerous game with a strong woman.

"Sawyer," she warned.

"It's a yes or no question," he said. "I know you heard me ask it."

"Actually, I don't think you ever did ask it."

"Will you marry me, Jeri Bell?"

Love ran through her eyes, and she said, "Yes."

Sawyer kissed her, this woman he loved so very much. She kissed him back, laughing and crying at the same time. He slipped the ring on her finger, and they both admired it. He didn't want to press her, but he had to know how long he had to wait to be with her again.

"What are you thinking for a date?" he asked.

"Well, if I start the house today, which I can't do, because I need to rent an excavator, I bet I could have it done in three or four months."

"I'm thinking August," he said, glancing at her. "Specifically, August eighteenth."

She sucked in a breath and looked at him. "Really?"

"My whole life changed the day you walked into my house instead of yours," he said. "And then again the day we got married. It's a good day. Something for us to celebrate."

Her face softened as she smiled. "All right. August eighteenth."

SAWYER FELT like he'd spent the last year waiting for things to happen. Of course, he kind of had. A few days until they could go to the office in Van Nuys and get married. A couple of months until her official contractor's license came in. Six months to get divorced.

And now, four months to get married again.

Each day passed, as time definitely did, and Sawyer found himself dressing up in a nice suit once again. This time, though, he and Jeri hadn't just had their first kiss and snuck off the ranch together.

She had gotten the marriage license again, but he'd asked Pastor Williams to come up to the ranch to marry them. His mother had taken care of all of the food, and they were feeding all the guests after the ceremony.

Scarlett had used the huge horse barn for her wedding, and Adele and Carson, who'd both returned to the ranch after the wedding in April, would be too.

Sawyer and Jeri had opted to set up their wedding right in front of their cabins. After all, that was where they'd spent the most time falling in love.

Guilt pumped through him with every heartbeat as he peeked outside to see Hudson, Carson, Cache, Dave, Lance, and Ames outside, struggling to set up the tents. It was so hot in California in August, and there wasn't much shade in the Cabin Community.

Two huge tents went up, and then Sawyer couldn't really see what was happening. Jeri had hired a party supply company for the tents, chairs, and tables, and she'd sketched everything out for him.

He knew intellectually what he'd find under the tents, and he thought of Jeri next door in her cabin, getting ready for their wedding. This time, she wasn't alone. Her mother and siblings had come, as had Randy and Pearl.

Jeri had involved his mother in a lot of the prep, and she was currently next door too. Sawyer stood in his house with his brother and his father, all of them ready to go. None of them talking.

Finally, his dad said, "I think I just saw your mother."

"Almost ready then," Sawyer said, so much more nervous this time than last time.

"I'm happy for you," his dad said. "I could tell there was something special between you and Jeri when you brought her to the picnic last year."

"Yeah?" Sawyer asked.

"Definitely." His dad hugged him. "Now, if we could just get James to propose to Peach, I wouldn't have to listen to your mother talk about it all the time." He flashed a smile at James, who held up both hands in an *I surrender* gesture.

"Hey, it's not up to me," he said, smiling. "I've asked her. She said she needs more time."

Sawyer frowned, a blip of concern moving through him. "More time? For what?"

James's smile slipped. "She's, uh, working through some things."

"I get that," Sawyer said.

"Yeah?"

"Definitely." Sawyer looked at his brother. "Just give her time."

Someone knocked on the front door, drawing Sawyer's attention there. His mother came in without waiting to be invited, and she gasped when she saw Sawyer. Tears filled her eyes, and she drew him into a tight hug that made Sawyer's emotions fly all over the place too.

"You two are perfection," she gushed. "You should see her dress. It's *gor-ge-ous*." She stepped back and brushed her hands down his lapels. "And you are the best looking man anywhere." She beamed at him, her dramatic personality perfect for weddings.

"Time to go," she said. "Everyone's here." She linked her arm through her husband's, and they led the way out.

Sawyer went down his front steps and took a few steps toward the altar that had been placed right on his front lawn. Blue lay down at his feet, already panting though there were misters and fans mounted in the corners of the tent.

He looked out over the sea of faces, finding all the ranch personnel he loved so much. Everyone was in place and ready—except Gramps and Jeri. Over the months of their engagement, she'd gone with him to visit Gramps, ultimately asking him to escort her down the aisle.

Maybe something had happened.

Fear and doubt struck him like lightning, and he looked at his mother, who swiveled her head around as if Jeri should've come out an hour ago and not just five minutes.

Scarlett stood up from her spot in the front row, and touched Sawyer's arm. "Let me go check. Be right back."

Sawyer wanted to call after her, get her to stop. Come back and reassure him that Jeri was going to come down the aisle and marry him. Or go inside in Scarlett's place. Then when he found out Jeri wasn't coming, he'd already be out of the spotlight. Away from the eyes.

A few minutes later, Scarlett came hurrying back toward him. She leaned into him and whispered, "Gramps brought the wrong shoes. They're coming now."

Relief spread through him, and he turned with everyone else when the wedding march started. There were no bridesmaids and no groomsmen. Just Jeri and Gramps, stepping slowly down the middle of all the people, one of her crazy chickens behind her.

Her dress was glorious and beautiful, with a tight bodice and then yards and yards of fabric that flowed down to the ground. She looked royal and majestic, and Sawyer's whole body went on alert.

The chicken squabbled, and Blue's ears perked up. Sawyer shushed him and told him to forget about the chicken while a few guests giggled. He forgot all about everything when Gramps passed Jeri to him and demanded a hug of his own.

Everyone laughed then, including Sawyer, and he was so glad he'd been able to have this wedding—if only for Gramps.

Scarlett came over and helped her grandfather to an empty seat beside her, and Jeri and Sawyer faced Pastor Williams.

"What a blessed event," he said, and this wedding was so different than their first. Peace filled Sawyer, and he listened with rapt attention as the pastor pronounced marriage blessings upon him and Jeri.

He said, "I do," when it was time, and when she did, a smile exploded onto Sawyer's face.

He'd kissed this bride before, but the second time was so much better than the first.

"For real," he whispered, kissing her again, the crowd cheering behind him.

"Always and forever," she whispered back, pressing her forehead to his.

"I love you," they said together, and Sawyer had never felt such joy.

Read on for a sneak peek at **LAST CHANCE REUNION**. You'll get to see why Dave never asks out Sissy, though he dates everyone else...

Sneak Peek! Last Chance Reunion - Chapter One

S issy Longston adjusted the temperature in the brand new administration building, the air conditioner actually working a little too well. She hadn't dressed for such chilly conditions, and she wished she had a sweater to put on.

To remedy her icy hands, she stepped outside into the brilliant California sunshine. May really was the most beautiful month in the state, and she faced east, out into the openness of Last Chance Ranch.

She took a deep breath, the good, earthy smell of the air clearing her mind. Well, at least a little. She worked long hours, yes, but she sure did love the ranch she'd landed at a couple of years ago.

She'd usually had a seething, insatiable need to move on after two or three years, but she didn't see that happening here. Maybe her gypsy heart and wandering spirit had finally found a place to call home.

She inhaled and exhaled again, her fingers and toes tingling as they warmed up beneath the sunshine. She pulled out her phone and logged into the dating app she'd started using a few months ago. She wasn't terribly active, and most of the time, men messaged her and she didn't get it for days.

But she'd been chatting with someone named Cowboy-Dan, and he'd asked her out three days ago. *Just dinner*, he'd said. *Nothing fancy. If it's a no, it's a no.*

She'd liked that he wasn't too terribly clingy, but she still hadn't answered him. The reason was Tom Rosser, the man she'd been out with a couple of times now. She hadn't spent a whole lot of her adult life dating, choosing instead to buy airplane tickets and travel the world, but she knew she couldn't go out with more than one man at a time.

Tom was good-looking and sweet, but the spark between them felt like one of those cheap fireworks children lit. Fire and pop for about fifteen seconds. Then just smoke, darkness, and a bad smell.

She tapped out a quick message to Tom, hoping to let him down easy. *I'm sorry. I don't think this is working out. Thanks for everything.*

Tom had bought her two meals and driven up to the ranch once to pick her up when her car wouldn't start. She'd had Hudson look at it since then, and it was humming along just fine now.

Sissy sighed, her head pounding, and she hoped she wasn't coming down with a summer cold. After all, there was nothing worse than being sick when the weather was good.

"Hey, Sissy," Amber called, and Sissy lifted her hand in a wave. Amber was a pretty woman who had taken to wearing a cowgirl hat whenever she wasn't in the volunteer building. Sissy had been going to goat yoga every morning for months, simply to be around people. She'd never had any problem fitting in, but she was starting to wonder if she'd been focusing on all the wrong things, for far too long.

She'd always put adventures and experiences above relationships. Having a home, a family, a husband had never been a priority—until now. And at forty-three-years-old, she feared she'd waited too long. Visited Greece one too many times when she should've gone out with Tanner Duplaix instead.

Or Dave Merrill. The thought poisoned her mind, and she tried to push it away. She and Dave had started at Last Chance Ranch in the same week, and she'd almost quit. But she'd liked Scarlett too much, and she had nowhere else to go. Her two weeks notice had already been put in at the corporation where she led the accounting department.

She didn't want a life in the city. So she'd stayed. Dave simply avoided her, and she didn't speak to him. Or look at him at ranch functions. If she saw him coming, she made a detour. It was a system that had worked for almost two years.

She knew she'd hurt him all those years ago. They'd been serious—diamond-ring serious—and she'd even worn his ring for a week before giving it back and breaking up with him.

She lost track of him after that, but the man wasn't stupid. He knew she'd gone back to her old boyfriend—not that that relationship had panned out. Sissy had disappeared to South America for a month after everything, and she'd come back to a different job. A new adventure.

Now, she was just tired.

She navigated to CowboyDan's message and said, *I'm free tonight. Doable?*

He didn't respond right away, and she went back inside to work through the budget for Horse Heaven. They'd gotten seven new equines from Forever Friends, and that meant several more mouths to feed.

Scarlett Adams, the owner of the ranch, trusted Sissy to approve budgets and make sure the ranch had enough money coming in to maintain animal care and staff salaries. She and her husband, Hudson, had worked tirelessly to make Last Chance Ranch into what it was, and the ranch, the animals, and the people who lived here were thriving.

Sissy didn't live on-site, but about three out of every five days, she wished she did. It warmed her heart to see so many people building lives here, and she'd witnessed three weddings last year. Scarlett and Hudson lived in the homestead, and everyone loved them.

Adele and Carson were the ranch's cutest couple, and

they lived in a tiny cabin next to Gramps on the edge of the homestead's lawn, and Sissy may or may not have had to fight off the jealousy every day as she drove by the house Jeri had built for her and her husband, Sawyer to live in.

The two-story beauty sat just a few feet inside the fences of the ranch, right on the main road, and Sissy had never wanted a house as much as she wanted that one. It was then that she'd realized she *did* want to be a wife, a mother, and a homeowner, all things she'd never done in her life.

Not even once.

The door to the administration building opened, and Sissy looked up from her desk though there was a lobby and she was working in her office. No one else worked here, though, so if someone had come, they'd come to see her.

She arrived in the lobby just as Dave said, "This is the admin building. Our accountant works here." He turned to leave, his eyes catching on hers.

They both froze. His voice had done that to her, and she watched the storm roll across the man's handsome features. It seemed impossible that she'd had a hold over his heart for all these years, but he scowled at her and added, "Here she is. Cecilia Longston."

The other cowboy with him stepped around Dave, and Sissy almost went into cardiac arrest. "Gray?" she asked.

"Oh, you two know each other?" Dave looked back and forth between Sissy and Gray as a smile spread across Gray's face.

"We sure do know each other," Gray said, swaggering forward and tucking his shirt into his jeans, though it was already tucked perfectly fine. "We went out two or three times a few years ago." Gray leaned against the desk in the lobby. "How are you, Sissy?"

"It was twice," Sissy clarified for Dave as well as Gray. "Five years ago. And I'm fine."

Dave's jaw clenched, and she wanted to make him relax. She'd do anything to get him to forgive her. Her heart wailed it was beating so fast under the weight of his glare.

"Gray's our new hire," Dave said, his voice definitely on the stiff side.

"And what will you be doing here at Last Chance Ranch?" Sissy asked.

"Agriculture specialist," he said as if he'd just been elected President of the United States.

"You have a degree in that, I believe," Sissy said, hearing the quick intake of air from Dave's direction. She looked at him, silently begging God and him to hear her prayer.

Please forgive me.

Help him to forgive me.

"That's right." Gray's gaze dripped down Sissy, and she didn't like it. Not one little bit.

"Well, we have to go," Dave said. "Loads more to see, man." He tapped Gray on the shoulder, glared one last dagger at Sissy, and turned to leave the building.

Gray lingered, and even went so far as to ask, "Are you single, Sissy? Want to go to dinner tonight?"

Dave spun back toward them, his whole face dark and dangerous. How he could make her heart pitter-patter still, all these years later, wasn't lost on her. They'd met when he was still active in the Army, and she'd fallen fast for him. Fast, and hard.

But she'd always had so many doubts, especially when she was younger, and she'd barely been twenty-five when Dave had proposed. She'd seen nothing of the world. Experienced nothing but college and a boring job in a boring No-Name Hollywood office.

Going back to Teddy had been a mistake. But Dave hadn't heard any of those explanations. Once she'd broken off their engagement, he'd cut off all contact.

"I'm busy tonight," she said with a smile, silently begging Gray to *just go. Please go.* "Sorry, Gray."

He knocked twice on the desk in front of him and opened his mouth to say something else.

Dave got to him first, saying, "Dude, come on. She's busy, and we've got other places to be."

Their eyes met again, and Sissy mouthed the words *Thank you* to him. Dave didn't react at all, other than to turn and walk out of the building, Gray behind him this time.

Sissy sagged into the doorframe, the adrenaline coursing through her the only thing keeping her upright.

But hey, progress—Dave had done something for her. Said her name without biting it off and spitting it out.

Her phone bleeped out the three-toned alert that she'd gotten a message on Christian Catch.

Sure, CowboyDan said. *I'm free tonight.*

Sissy smiled at the message, turning to go back into her office, glad the air conditioner had stopped blowing. She spent the next twenty minutes making arrangements to meet CowboyDan in a red sweater at a popular bistro in Pasadena, close to where she lived.

She never met men anywhere but Scooter's, as she knew a couple of waitresses there, and they were always busy.

With a date with a new man—someone she'd had good online conversations with—on the horizon, she managed to put both Dave and Gray out of her mind.

For a few minutes, at least.

Then Dave came roaring back, just like he had been for eighteen years now.

Sneak Peek! Last Chance Reunion - Chapter Two

David Merrill had drawn the way short stick when he'd been assigned to take Gray Lennox around the ranch. He hated the tours in general, but this guy was a real piece of work. He'd flirted with every woman he'd come in contact with, making Dave—who'd been out with fifteen women in the past two years—seem like he never got off the ranch.

As he sweated beneath his cowboy hat, Gray sauntered along next to him. "Does she have a boyfriend?"

Dave employed all of his patience. "Not that I'm aware of."

"She and I, we did go out," Gray said, as if Dave had challenged him on the point.

"Congratulations," Dave said, unwilling to get into a game of who was better between the two of them. Dave had dated Sissy for eight months before asking her to marry him. She'd cried and kissed him, and he could still feel the way she fit perfectly in his arms.

The anger he carried wasn't healthy, and he knew it. It had been a very long time, and while he'd gotten over Sissy, moved on, dated other people, he'd never gotten married. Never asked another woman to marry him.

And he'd lost serious girlfriends because of it. Two of them had actually accused him of having commitment issues, which he supposed he did.

On their way to Horse Heaven, he pulled out his phone and messaged BrainyGirl, the woman he'd been messaging through the Christian dating app he'd found about a month ago. Not that Dave had trouble getting a date. He'd been out with over a dozen women, most of them from right here at Last Chance Ranch.

He wasn't looking for serious. He had band practice a couple of times a week, and he wanted to be social in the evenings. It wasn't a crime to ask a woman to dinner or a movie, have someone to spend his down time with.

He didn't hold hands with everyone, and he hadn't kissed any of the last several women he'd been out with.

When he'd first come to Last Chance Ranch, he'd told Sawyer he didn't want to be set up, and he was fine on his own. Both were true. He had no problem getting his own dates, and he simply didn't want to get married.

Even if the bride were Sissy?

But the bride will never be Sissy, he argued with himself. So it's a moot point.

"Do you think I could ask her out again?" Gray asked.

"Sissy?" Dave scoffed, his thumbs flying over the screen to make plans with BrainyGirl. "I don't know why you'd want to, but sure. Ask her out."

"You don't like her?"

"It's...she's fine," he said, unwilling to say anything too negative about her. "She's not my type, but hey, if you liked her, by all means, ask her out." Just the thought of Sissy going out with Gray made his blood boil, and he had no right to feel that way.

She'd made it quite clear how she felt about him, breaking their relationship right in half, even though she'd cried. Then she'd left town, and Dave had to find out through a mutual friend that she'd gone right back to the boyfriend she'd had before they'd started dating.

That had hurt the most. He'd wanted to march right to her house, pound on the door, and demand to know what she was thinking. But he'd been stationed in Virginia at the time, and that was a long way from California.

He finished making his date with the woman he'd been getting to know online, hoping she'd be as charming in real life as she was on the screen.

"There you are," Hudson said, and Dave shoved his phone in his back pocket. "You must be Gray."

"Hudson Flannigan," Dave said. "He's the foreman over Horse Heaven."

"Dave's over the llamas," Hudson said. "He tell you that?"

"We haven't made it to LlamaLand yet," Dave said.

"And he's a bit sore he didn't get the dogs." Hudson grinned at Dave like it was so funny he'd wanted Canine Club and had lost the game of rock, paper, scissors to Cache. The man already had his hands full with the cattle, and Dave got assigned as second-in-command over the canines. So it was still acceptable to him.

Lance Longcomb was foreman over Piggy Paradise, and Adele had domain over Feline Frenzy. Amber Haws ran the volunteer programs, as well as did goat yoga. But Adele's husband, Carson took care of the goats in the Goat Grounds.

Sawyer and Jeri took care of the chickens, and Sawyer worked wherever Hudson needed him most. Dave got him a lot of the time in LlamaLand, and he really liked Sawyer. He and Jeri were off the ranch for a few days while they went down to a hospital in Los Angeles to pick up the baby boy they were adopting.

"I need someone out at the cemetery later this week," Hudson said, glancing between Dave and Gray.

"I'll do it," Dave said, because Gray couldn't go off on his own so soon. Not only that, but Dave loved going out to the remote cabin about an hour's ride from the epicenter of the ranch. He liked laying on his back as the stars came to life, and he liked walking through the pet cemetery and thinking about the people who'd buried their pets at Last Chance Ranch.

"I just need a report by Monday," he said. "I want at least two sections mapped."

"Yes, sir," Dave said, though Hudson hated being called sir. Maybe he shouldn't bark so many orders, the way Dave's military sergeants did, and he grinned at Hudson, who rolled his eyes.

"Gray, you'll be with the chickens until Sawyer and Jeri get back." Hudson looked down at the clipboard in his hand. "Karla will have lunch today, and Dave, Gramps wants you to bring your new dog by for a visit." Hudson looked up. "We're moving horses from pasture six to pasture three today, and then Dave, you're free to LlamaLand."

Dave nodded and pulled on a pair of leather gloves. "How many horses?"

"Sixteen." Hudson turned and hung the clipboard on the nail by the door before putting on his own gloves. "Where are you from, Gray?"

"Marietta," he said. "It's inland a bit. Nice place."

Dave listened with one ear, wondering when Sissy had been in Southern California, an hour from the beach. That didn't sound like her at all, but Dave supposed he didn't know who she was anymore. Nearly two decades had passed since their romance, and a keen sense of missing pounded through his bloodstream he wished wouldn't.

The only way he'd been able to get her out of his system

was through work. He put his head down and got the job done, and that pushed Sissy into the recesses of his mind, where she belonged.

That evening, he showered all the llama and horse smells off his body and out of his hair. BrainyGirl had wanted to go out that night, and Dave didn't have other plans. It had taken her a couple of days to answer him, but he didn't mind. Their relationship was casual, easy. He'd learned she liked chocolate croissants and staying up late.

He was more of a morning person, but he would eat anything with chocolate in it—especially Adele's peanut butter bars. The woman was a genius in the kitchen, and in addition to hanging out with the goats and taking care of over sixty cats, she ran a social media foodie channel. He and the other cowboys were always more than happy to eat her leftovers, and Carson almost always had something with chocolate in it on the workbench in the hay barn.

Hudson had put a mini fridge out there too, and everyone knew if you needed a snack, you checked the hay barn before going home.

Dave certainly didn't have great food at home. His time in the Army and his many years as a bachelor meant he *could* cook for himself. He just didn't want to.

He dressed in clean jeans and a blue T-shirt with the

word ARMY across the front in big, blocky letters. It would give him and BrainyGirl something to talk about. Dave didn't normally have a problem making conversation, especially if the food was good.

She'd suggested Scooter's, an upscale bistro he'd eaten at several times over the past year or so. He liked their jalapeño poppers, and their clam chowder was the best in Pasadena. He'd agreed readily, because the service was fast and the place was always busy. That alone would make a bad date just fine, and if things were going well, he'd suggest a walk around the nearby Balboa Park.

BrainyGirl had said she'd be wearing a red sweater, but there wasn't a woman in the waiting area wearing anything of the sort. Had she gotten a table already? He was five minutes early, already regretting the choice of restaurants because of the pounding music.

He couldn't wait for the silence and tranquility of the outer cabin, the lazy day walking through the pet cemetery.

And that was when he realized his life had reached a new low. His idea of a good time was wandering through a pet cemetery?

Please let this date go well, he thought. While he didn't really want to settle down, the constant revolving door of women was getting tiring. His plan wasn't working anyway.

Sissy hadn't been jealous of any of his dates. She hadn't even seemed to care. And none of them had helped clear her from his head.

Maybe BrainyGirl will, he thought. He had a good feeling about her, and he stepped up to the hostess station so he could see into the bistro better.

"Can I help you?" a woman asked, and he looked right into the eyes of a woman he'd been out with last year.

A trickle of embarrassment ran through him. "Hailey," he said. "I didn't know you worked here."

She smiled at him, but not in the flirtatious way that had prompted him to ask her out. "It's only been a couple of months. Let me guess—you're meeting someone."

"Yes," he said.

"What's her name?"

"Uh...BrainyGirl."

Hailey's eyes widened. "So you don't know her real name?" The incredulity in her voice caused a passing waitress to pause. "Kirsten, he's here for BrainyGirl."

The blonde looked down to Dave's boot tips and back to his face. "You're kidding."

"I feel like I'm missing something," Dave said. "Is she here?" He stood taller than the women, but he couldn't see a flash of red anywhere.

"He doesn't know who she is," Hailey said.

"Which means she doesn't know who he is," Kirsten said. They seemed to have forgotten he stood there.

"Excuse me," he said, maybe with a little too much force. Both women startled and looked at him, almost like he was a ghost. "Is she here?"

The two women exchanged another glance, and then Kirsten said, "Yeah, she's here. I'll take you back."

Dave followed her, trying to riddle through what had just happened while simultaneously searching the restaurant for that red sweater. He finally saw it, in a booth in the back corner of the farthest room. It was literally the table with the longest walk in and out, but Dave didn't mind.

This woman had long, dark hair which curled softly over her shoulders. The sweater was definitely red, and it was sleeveless, revealing tan arms.

"Right there," Kirsten said, and Dave stepped past her, his heart beating too fast in his chest.

As if drawn by his approach, the woman turned to face him.

He froze, his pulse womping him with the force of gravity. It actually hurt as it radiated through his body.

"Sissy?" he said.

The woman who'd been plaguing him for many long years slid to the end of the booth and stood up. She wore a mixture of emotions on her face, ranging from disgust to acceptance to...hope? That couldn't be right.

She folded her arms and asked, "You're CowboyDan?"

He couldn't even nod. All he could think was that God certainly had a sick sense of humor.

Or maybe He was simply trying to shove Dave into the place where he should be. It was a toss-up at this point, especially as Sissy continued to stand there and stare at him, no smile in sight.

Oh, boy...this should be interesting! **Read LAST CHANCE REUNION today!**

Scan the QR code for a direct link to the paperback.

Last Chance Ranch Romance series

Journey to Last Chance Ranch and meet curvy, mature women looking for love later in life. Experience sisterhood, goat yoga, and a fake marriage against a stunning, inspirational ranch background—and some sexy cowboys too— from USA Today bestseller and Top 10 Kindle All-Star author Liz Isaacson!

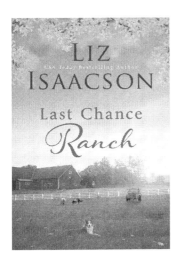

Last Chance Ranch (Book 1): A cowgirl down on her luck hires a man who's good with horses and under the hood of a car. Can Hudson fine tune Scarlett's heart as they work together? Or will things backfire and make everything worse at Last Chance Ranch?

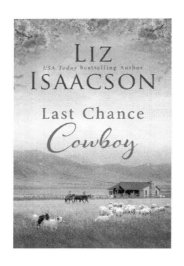

Last Chance Cowboy (Book 2): A billionaire cowboy without a home meets a woman who secretly makes food videos to pay her debts...Can Carson and Adele do more than fight in the kitchens at Last Chance Ranch?

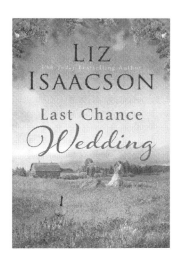

Last Chance Wedding (Book 3): A female carpenter needs a husband just for a few days... Can Jeri and Sawyer navigate the minefield of a pretend marriage before their feelings become real?

Last Chance Reunion (Book 4): An Army cowboy, the woman he dated years ago, and their last chance at Last Chance Ranch... Can Dave and Sissy put aside hurt feelings and make their second chance romance work?

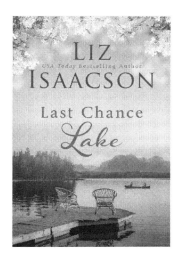

Last Chance Lake (Book 5): A former dairy farmer and the marketing director on the ranch have to work together to make the cow cuddling program a success. But can Karla let Cache into her life? Or will she keep all her secrets from him - and keep *him* a secret too?

Last Chance Christmas (Book 6): She's tired of having her heart broken by cowboys. He waited too long to ask her out. Can Lance fix things quickly, or will Amber leave Last Chance Ranch before he can tell her how he feels?

About Liz

Liz Isaacson writes inspirational romance, usually set in Texas, or Montana, or anywhere else horses and cowboys exist. She lives in Utah, where she walks her dogs daily, watches a lot of Netflix, and eats a lot of peanut butter M&Ms while writing. Find her on her website at feelgood-fictionbooks.com.